Seven Tales in Amber

Seven Tales in Amber

by Roger Zelazny

Acknowledgments

"Introduction" copyright © 2019 by Warren Lapine.

"Prologue to Trumps Of Doom" originally appeared in *Trumps of Doom* Underwood Miller 1985. Copyright © 1985 by The Amber Corporation.

"A Secret of Amber" originally appeared in *Amberzine* #12-15, 2005. Copyright © 2005 by Ed Greenwood.

"Salesman's Tale" originally appeared in *Amberzine* #6, February 1996. Copyright © 1996 by The Amber Corporation.

"Blue Horse, Dancing Mountains" originally appeared in *Wheel of Fortune*, AvoNova 1995. Copyright © 1995 by The Amber Corporation.

"The Shroudling and the Guisel" originally appeared in *Realms of Fantasy* #1, October 1994. Copyright © 1994 by The Amber Corporation.

"Coming to a Cord" originally appeared in *Pirate Writings* #7, Summer 1995. Copyright © 1995 by The Amber Corporation.

"Hall of Mirrors" originally appeared in *Castle Fantastic*, Daw 1996. Copyright © 1996 by The Amber Corporation.

Table of Contents

Introduction

I owe Roger Zelazny a great debt, one which I can never truly repay. Roger Zelazny completely changed my life, twice.

When I was eleven my parents had a financial setback and we moved into one of the worse neighborhoods in our town. I immediately fell in with the wrong crowd and while I didn't exactly get into a lot of trouble it wasn't for want of effort. Not one of my friends from that neighborhood made it to college.

As I recall I was the only reader amongst the group. The first science fiction book I ever owned was given to me by one of those friends who stole it just because he could. Once stolen he had no use for it. Since I was the only person he knew who enjoyed reading he gave it to me.

The book was *Destination Universe* by A. E. Van Vogt. That was my introduction to science fiction; I was 12. At 12 I wanted to quit school, but as my mother pointed out it was against state law for me to drop out until I was 16. So I grudgingly went to school most days, skipped others, and was uninterested in any kind of employment. Hanging out with my friends in the park doing stupid things was all I was interested in, but I still enjoyed reading. and now I was reading some science fiction in addition to the history and mystery books I'd been reading up to that point.

Then one day, my parents got a bit of junk mail from Publisher's Clearing House. One of its offerings was a charter subscription to a shiny new magazine. *Isaac Asimov's Science Fiction Magazine*. Asimov was a name I knew from the middle school library. I asked my mother to get me a subscription. She refused as I wasn't much help around the house and had a terrible attitude.

But I really wanted that magazine, so I offered that if she'd get me the subscription I'd go to the newspaper and see if I could get a paper route and pay her back. If that didn't work I'd clean the house for a month. She agreed. I filled out the forms and stuck all the stickers in the proper places and dropped it into the mail on my way to the *Greenfield Recorder,* which promptly gave me a paper route. I paid my mother back after my first payday and the magazine arrived shortly thereafter. I enjoyed the magazine; it wasn't life changing, but I liked it.

Inevitably the Science Fiction Book Club rented my name from *Asimov's*. As I recall I was about to quit my paper route as I was not enjoying the experience. But the enticement of 4 free books, and omnibus editions at that, was enough for me to decide to keep the job until I had at least purchased the 4 additional books I was obligating myself to buy. As I recall I chose *The Foundation Trilogy* by Isaac Asimov, *The Dragonriders of Pern* by Anne McCaffrey, *The Complete Enchanter* by Fletcher Pratt and L. Sprague de Camp, and, of course, *The Chronicles of Amber Volume I and Volume II.*

I remember reading the descriptions of the books over and over again while I awaited their arrival. Even then there was something about the description of the Amber books that captivated me. Even so, or perhaps because of this, I saved the Amber books for last. Reading those first three omnibus editions one after the other during a single weekend was an amazing experience. It quickly became clear to me that from here on out I was only going to read science fiction and fantasy as nothing else that I'd ever read had captivated me as much as these books had.

But as it turned out I was only getting started. The Amber books riveted me to my core. The preceding books made me want to read more science fiction, but Zelazny made me want to write it. With my next paper route money I purchased a used typewriter and several used books by Roger Zelazny. I didn't realize it yet, but my life had just changed dramatically for the better.

My dad was a sand-mixer at a foundry. There's nothing wrong with that, but that was the direction my life had been heading in up until I encountered Roger Zelazny and the Chronicles of Amber. With no inclination to further my education and no aspirations beyond sliding through life as easily as I could, I wasn't on a trajectory to have much of a life. Fortunately, I realized that if I wanted to be a writer I'd need stronger writing skills, and I set out to acquire those skills. My grades immediately picked up, and over the course of my 8th grade year my teachers slowly moved me off of the middle-of-the-road track I'd been on and into the college bound track. Being in classes with a different group of kids meant that my social circle also began to slowly changed.

A year after discovering Amber, my life was completely different. I ended up finishing high school rather than dropping out, and I went on to major in English at the University of Massachuset. At 27 I started a science fiction magazine. Roger Zelazny had had a fanzine so it seemed like a path I should follow. I started my zine just as the desktop revolution hit, so I was able to kick it up a notch or two beyond what had been possible even a few years earlier, so my zine quickly had national distribution.

The first issue of my first magazine, despite having a terrible name made enough of an impression on the field that name writers started sending me submissions. I also started getting invitations to science fiction conventions. At conventions I was able to meet writers and network, which in turn helped the quality of the magazine. But I really did it more to meet my heroes than anything else.

At some Northeast convention or another I found a flyer for a small convention in Lynchburg, Virginia, called Kaleidoscope. I wouldn't have paid it any attention, it being twelve hours from home, but the guest of honor was Roger Zelazny. I found a phone number and called the convention to see if I could get on the programing. I didn't hold out much hope as the convention was the following weekend.

To my surprise and delight the con-chair seemed quite happy to add me as a last minute program participant. He even offered to put me on all of Roger's panels, which I quickly accepted. I put together some interview questions in the hopes that I might get to interview Roger for my magazine. Several days later I drove the 12 hours south to attend the convention.

As it turned out it was the smallest convention I had ever attended. I arrived somewhat early in the day and met the con-chair after checking into my room at the hotel. He asked me if I'd like to meet Roger before the con started. I quickly said yes and I found myself carrying a box of comic books back to his house in the place of a gopher who wasn't a Zelazny fan. As I recall Roger was coming towards the door as we were coming in and the box of comic books I was carrying chose that moment to essentially explode and send comics flying about the entryway. I immediately started picking them up and putting them back into their box as did Roger. Once all the comics were back in the box Roger extended his had and said, "Hello, I'm Roger Zelazny, pleased to meet you." I took his hand and shook it, it was one of only two moments in my life that I went full on fan boy.

Later I was back at the convention hanging out in the lobby of the hotel. Since I was new to the field and out of my geographical region I didn't know anyone there. I remember I had struck up a conversation with Jim Zimmerman, an aspiring artist who was every bit the Zelazny fan I was. While we were talking, a woman in a slinky black dress entered the hotel; Jim pointed her out to me and said, "Wow, look at her."

I had to agree she was one of the most attractive women I'd ever seen. See locked eyes with me as she walked towards the check-in desk. I remember thinking *I have to find some excuse to talk with her*, and then I thought, *if she doesn't stop looking at me she's going to walk into that potted palm tree, I'm going to laugh, and she's never going to talk to me.* And indeed, she walked right into the palm tree. I almost managed not to laugh. But when I ran into a couple hours later and asked her if she was okay she laughed and said, "Nothing hurt but my pride." I didn't know it then, but I'd be dating this beauty within a year, marry her within five years, and start a family with her within ten years. Twenty-four years later and we're still happily married. Had Roger Zelazny not been the GoH of the convention I'd have never met her. That was the second time Roger changed my life for the better.

Later that day I interviewed Roger for an interview that appeared in *Absolute Magnitude* #1, which was actually the third issue of the magazine, but as I said it started life with a terrible name and we changed it with the third issue. During the interview I found out that Roger was unhappy with the people who had agreed to publish a book of his poetry. I assured him that if the deal didn't work out I'd be more than happy to publish it. Long story short, the deal fell through, Roger called me, and I agreed to publish his *A Hymn to the Sun*.

A bit later that year Roger offered me the Amber short story "Coming to a Cord," which I had to turn down as *Absolute Magnitude* only published hard science fiction. He asked if I could recommend a market for it as he had several stories, planned to write more, and he wanted to get them all published that year so he could release them as a collection. I suggested *Pirate Writings*, which is where it eventually appeared.

Saying no to an Amber story was the hardest thing I've ever done in my literary career, but I was certain that now that I'd be publishing Roger's poetry book that he'd send me a story I could use soon enough. I wish I'd known he was never going to be able to offer me another story. I would have broken my rule and published it.

I remember being numb when I got the news that Roger had passed. I couldn't imagine that I'd never read anything new from him again. I was glad that I'd decided to tell him my story and that I owed him my life as it were. I remember he seemed quite touched by it and I thought about that and cried. I didn't get to know him as well as I would have liked, and yet no one else has ever impacted my life in quite such a profound way.

The book you hold in your hands has magic in it. The magic of Amber, a magic that can change lives and alter the course of history. As you turn the pages, remember it's never too late to live your best life. I have Roger Zelazny and Amber to thank for mine.

Prologue to *Trumps Of Doom*

It was almost too easy. A turning, a twisting, a doubling back . . .

And then he faced a rough, slanted wall, looked up and saw the shaft. He commenced climbing.

It was no longer easy. A swaying sensation began—faint, then distinct—as if he were mounting into the uppermost branches of a tall tree. His way brightened end then dimmed, repeatedly, in no perceptible pattern. After a time, his eyes ached. Images doubled, wavered . . .

When the way grew suddenly level he doubted his vision, till his extended hand assured him that there was indeed a choice of passages.

He leaned and moved his head into each of these. The faint musical sound seemed slightly louder in the one to the left, and he followed it. Of that, at least, he was certain.

Now his way rose and fell. He climbed up, he climbed down. The brightening and dimming continued, only now the brightness was brighter and the dimness dimmer.

And the sensations of external movement had not abated. The floor of the tunnel seemed to ripple beneath his feet, the walls and roof to contract and expand. He stumbled, caught himself. Stumbled again . . .

At the next turning the sounds grew slightly louder, and he realized that they were not a tune, but rather a totally random concatenation of noises.

He climbed. He descended. The passageway shrank, and finally he crawled.

The sensations of movement increased. At times he seemed to be spinning; other times, it felt as if he were falling into an enormous abyss.

The flashes of light now drove nails of pain into skull. He began to hallucinate. Faces and figures. Flames. Or were they hallucinations?

He felt the first faint pulsation upon his left wrist . . .

How long had he been moving? His clothes were already in tatters and he bled, painlessly, from a dozen scrapes and lacerations.

He descended a well and emerged somehow upward onto a floor. Mad laughter rang about him, ceasing only when he realized it to be his own.

The sounds grew even louder, until it lefts as if he negotiated a gallery of demonic bells—wild, out of phase, their vibrations beating against him.

Thinking became painful. He knew that he must not stop, that he must not turn back, that he must not take any of the lesser turnings where the sounds came softer. Any of these courses would prove fatal. He reduced this to one imperative: Continue.

Again, a pulsing at his wrist, and a faint, slow movement . . .

He gritted his teeth when he saw that he must climb once more, for his limbs had grown heavy. Each movement seemed as if it were performed underwater—slowly, requiring more than normal effort.

A screen of smoke offered frightening resistance. He drove himself against it for an age before he passed through and felt his movement become easy once again. Six times this occurred, and each time the pressure against him was greater.

When he crawled out, drooling and dripping blood, on the other side of the chamber from which he had entered, his eyes darted wildly and could not fix upon the small, dark figure which stood before him.

"You are a fool," it told him.

It took some time for the words to register, and when they did he lacked the strength with which to reply.

"A lucky fool," it went on, darkness flowing about it like wings. (Or were they really wings?) "I had not judged you ready to essay the Logrus for a long while yet."

He closed his eyes against this speaker, and an image of the route he had followed danced within his mind's seeing, like a bright, torn web folding in a breeze.

" . . . And a fool not to have borne a blade and so enchanted it . . . or a mirror, a chalice, or a wand to brace your magic. No, all I see is a piece of rope. You should have waited, for more instruction, for greater strength. What say you?"

He raised himself from the floor, and a mad light danced within his eyes.

"It was time," he said. "I was ready."

"And a cord! What a half-ass—uck!"

The cord, glowing now, tightened about his throat.

When the other released it, the dark one coughed and nodded.

"Perhaps you knew what you were doing—on that count . . . " it muttered. "Is it really time? You will be leaving?"

"Yes."

A dark cloak fell upon his shoulders. He heard the splash of water within a flask.

"Here."

As he drank, the cord wrapped itself about his wrist and vanished.

"Thanks, Uncle." he said, after several swallows. The dark figure shook its head. "Impulsive," it said. "Just like your father."

A Secret of Amber

With Ed Greenwood

"It was starting to end," the book—THE book—began. Mildly interested (my father's study was chock-full of all sorts of books, and each new opening of pages might reveal just about anything), I read on. By "Where the hell was I?" I was hooked.

Let thirty-some years blow past, and come to a standstill now. On a height, looking down into Arden, with a silver blade in one hand and the cold tingling of Trumps in the other.

I'm still hooked. I think I always will be. I want to believe that Amber is real, and that this place is just a Shadow.

Over those years, I read and re-read Nine Princes In Amber—and as each new novel came out, I and my best friend Dave devoured them, walked the parks near our homes for hours speculating as to who among the Royals was behind what attack, and making untrustworthy alliance with whom.

I wrote my own books. I dared to travel to SF conventions. There came a day when a man with glasses as severe as my own sat at a table, signing the books a long line of fans thrust eagerly at him. I was one of them, and the book was my father's precious copy of Nine Princes in Amber.

And he swung it open at my bookmark.

My bookmark, foolishly left inside. 'Foolishly' because it bore these words of mine:

*

She raised an eyebrow. "I thought better of you, brother. It seems I was wrong."

I sipped my wine. "It seems you were. Again."

Silence. She raised the other brow.

I gave her more silence.

"Well. Corwin?"

"Disappointment," I observed, over the rim of my glass, "is a beast that runs in packs."

*

Seven Tales in Amber

And the Lord of Amber looked up from my scribbles and smiled. "Fiona," he said.
It was not a question, but I nodded and grinned like an idiot. He flashed me a grin
just as wide, and wrote:

*

"Whereas wit is a bird that eludes the hand of rather too many princes."

I shrugged. "Your disapproval concerns me even less than usual, Fi. All things considered."

She tossed her head, red hair like a fall of flame. "Yet perhaps it should. All things considered."

I did things with my own eyebrows, emptied my glass, swung my boots down from the table, and headed for the door.

She chuckled, behind me.

I stopped, refrained from turning, and waited. Fiona could never resist showing the rest of us that she was a step ahead. Or pretending to be.

"You are wearing your blade," she said. "Good."

I went out, uttering no clever comments. With at least three murderous ghosts stalking Castle Amber, the time for such things was past.

*

He looked up from hand book and bookmark back to me, and laughed when he saw
my badge, and my name on it.

"Yes," I mumbled, "I'd been meaning to speak to you about that. The hospital—"

"Let you out for the day. Glad you came." Again the smile.

"Well, uh, thanks. See you next year," I said, and meant it.

He never signed the book, I realized later, but I had that precious bookmark—and
an idea. I thought long and hard, and then carefully wrote under Roger's words:

*

Lightning struck Kolvir, somewhere outside the windows, as I made my way back to my room. I saw no one.

There was a fire going on the grate, and everything was as I had left it. Which meant drink of my choosing was handy. I chose generously.

Full of good spirits, I cracked a better book and waited for whatever spirits might come.

Roger Zelazny

*

Let a year blow by, more than one, but in time there was another con, and another table, and Roger's latest, glossy and new. I handed it to him open, with the bookmark in it.

He looked up at me with an almost fierce grin, looked down again to read what I'd written, and then wrote under it:

*

It was very late, or rather early, before one of the walls opened in a place where it should not have done, and something that was both silver and shadow joined me.

Grayswandir felt good in my hand as I put down what I was finished drinking anyway, and waited.

Patience, they say, is chiefly a virtue for statues, but I'd made more than my share of mistakes, thus far, and blood is hell to get out of good rugs.

Came a whisper, out of darkness: "Corwin. Is it time?"

*

Another year, another new Amber book, and by then I'd penned my feeble few under Roger's:

*

So it knew me. You have the advantage, and all that. Time for what?

"No," I said very firmly. "Go away."

A stirring of silver, rising before me. "I fear not, Prince of Amber. I must have the blood I came for." The whisper was close, and hungry, and utterly unfamiliar.

I stepped back, slicing the air before me with my blade. "Suppose you tell me why. And your name, while you're at it."

The reply was a chuckle that did seem familiar, somehow, in the moment before the shadows boiled up into half a dozen stabbing, slashing blades, and Grayswandir rang in protest, sparks flying around me.

I considered some obscenities and then discarded them all.

Fiona had been ahead of me. Again.

"The Fool Prince," she'd called me once. And would again, if I was lucky

19

enough in these next few panting minutes. Or swift enough.

Lightning struck the Castle, somewhere nearby. Which itself should not have happened, what with the enchantments—

A swordpoint melted back into shadow, and then another, and my blade bit into nothing beyond.

A nothing that spilled silver out across my floor, scorching the rugs with sudden plumes of smoke.

"Prince of Amber!" my visitor hissed in pain. "You fight well!"

I struck again.

*

A handful of years, and another con, both of us visibly older now, but the grin as sharp as ever.

Roger sat back to read the whole thing through, this time, then reached out and shook my hand. Then without a pause he wrote:

*

And shadows fled before me, and I was alone.

My book was on the floor, blackened. Damn. I watched lightning flicker and wondered if I would ever know what I fought, or why. Family politics seemed as tiresome as ever.

Three ghosts, Benedict had said, and had been on the brink of saying more ere his face had smoothed and he'd turned away. Which meant he'd recognized the one he'd seen.

So had the lamplighter, before the ghost that slew him caught up with him and burned his skull bare, from within.

Coln had died, before that, and one of the cooks. Seven maids, or more by now, since.

Then they'd started on us. Flora had almost fallen to one, and then Julian. Almost.

We're tough meat, we of Amber.

*

I laughed at that, and so did he. I went home and pondered for some months before I wrote:

Roger Zelazny

*

My wall was as solid as ever, so I got out a lantern, and went looking for trouble. Something Princes of Amber never do, according to one of Droppa's little ditties.

Ho ho.

"Do not be too hasty," Dad had told me once, when I'd broken something in a rage at Eric. But then, a lot had changed since Dad's disappearance.

A lot, indeed. I was descending a stair when shadows and silver spun up again. Below me and above me, to the accompaniment of ghostly laughter.

I sighed. It was going to be one of those nights.

*

And when next our paths seemed fated to cross, it was to be at a GenCon where Roger Zelazny was to be Guest of Honor, and I'd be on my usual panels, plus one with him.

I was looking forward to a pleasant hour or so of passing that bookmark—two panels long, now, and I planned to bring more with me—back and forth along the table as we answered questions and held gentle debate, and really getting into the tale.

Our own little foray into Amber. May I have this dance, please? Yes, I'll have the same again, thanks!

But whatever gods there be had other ideas. Roger never made it into the summer, and now I'll never know how it would have turned out.

Damn it all.

But thank you, Roger. Thank you.

Thank you, Lord of Amber.

Ed Greenwood is the creator of the Forgotten Realms. He began writing in 1967. He created the Forgotten Realms Campaign Setting for his own D&D games in 1975, and its popularity with other gamers through *Dragon Magazine* led to TSR's purchase of the setting in 1986. He is the President and Publisher at The Ed Greenwood Group.

Salesman's Tale

Glad I'd planned on leaving Merlin in the Crystal Cave for a long while. Glad he didn't stay the entire time. As I interrupted our trumped conversation by kicking over my glass of iced tea and shouting "Shit! I spilled it—" I turned over the Trump of Doom in my good hand.

Junkyard Forest. Nice sketch, that. Though it didn't matter what it depicted, which is why I'd had Merlin fan the cards face down and had drawn one at random. That was for show, to confuse the Pattern. All of them led to places within spitting distance of the Crystal Cave—which had been the real reason for their existence in the first place. Their only purpose had been to draw Merlin into the Cave's orbit, at which point a blue crystal warning system was to have alerted me. The plan was for me to get there in a hurry and find a way to make him a prisoner.

Unfortunately, I hadn't gotten the message when he'd drawn the Sphinx to escape from mom. Her neurotoxins had canceled a necessary trigger signal from his nervous system—just one of the many ways she's messed up my plans without half-trying. Didn't matter, though, in the long run. I got Merlin there, anyway. Only . . . everything changed after that.

"Luke! You fool!" The Pattern's message blasted through me like the closing number at a rock concert. But the Junkyard Forest had already come clear, and I was trumping out, before the Pattern realized that tea rather than my blood was flowing upon it.

I rose to my feet as the Pattern faded, and I moved forward amid the rusty sawblade bushes, the twisted girder trees, the gaily colored beds of broken bottles. I began to run, blood spilling from the slashed palm of my left hand. I didn't even take the time to bind it. Once the Pattern recovered from its shock and discovered itself undamaged, it was going to begin scanning Shadow for me, for the others. They'd be safe within the ambit of the other Pattern, and that left me. The walls of the Crystal Cave had the effect of blocking every paraphysical phenomenon I'd been able to test them for, and

Seven Tales in Amber

I'd a hunch they'd screen me from the Pattern's scrutiny as well. It was just a matter of my getting there before it shadow-shuffled this far.

I increased my pace. I'd stayed in shape. I could run. Past rusting cars and swirls of bedsprings, broken tiles, shattered crates . . . Down alleys of ashes, up trails of bottlecaps and pulltabs . . . Alert. Waiting. Waiting for the world to spin and waver, to hear the voice of the Pattern announce, "Gotcha!"

I rounded a bend and caught a glimpse of blue in the distance. The Junkyard Forest—result of an ancient Shadow storm—ended abruptly as I entered upon a downward slope, to be succeeded within paces by a wood of the more normal variety.

Here, I heard a few birdcalls as I passed, and the humming of insects, above the steady striking of my feet upon the earth. The sky was overcast, and I could tell nothing of temperature or wind because of my activity. The shimmering mound of blue grew larger. I maintained my pace. By now, the others should be safe, if they'd made it at all. Hell! By now they should be well out of harm's way. Just a little while in this time-stream was a much longer time back on the main drag. They could be sitting around eating and joking by now. Even napping. I bit back a curse to save breath. That also meant that the Pattern could have been searching for even longer than it seemed . . . . Larger, even larger now, the blue ridge. I decided to see how well my finishing spurt had held up, and I went into high gear and held it there.

The earth and air were vibrated by what seemed a rumble of thunder. It could be a reaction of the irate design on having finally located me. I could also just be a rumble of thunder.

I kept pumping, and moments later, it seemed, I was braking so as not to smash up against that crystal base. No lightning bolts yet, and I scrambled for hand and toeholds—never having tried climbing this face of it before—as my lungs worked like a bellows and a light rain began to fall, mingling with a layer of my perspiration. I left bloody smears on the stone, but that should soon wash away.

Achieving the summit, I rushed to its opening on all fours and entered feet first, hanging, then dropping into the dark interior despite the presence of a ladder. Haste was all. Not until I stood within that shadowy blueness, still puffing, did I feel at all safe. As soon as I caught my breath I allowed myself to laugh. I had done it. I had escaped the Pattern. I walked about the chamber beating upon my thighs and slapping the walls. A victory such as this tasted good, and I would not let it pass unmarked. I hustled back to the larder, located a bottle of wine, opened it, and took a drink. Then I repaired to a side cavern which still contained a sleeping bag, seated myself upon it, and continued to chuckle as I reenacted in my mind our experience there at the primal Pattern. My lady Nayda had been so magnificent. So had Merlin, for that matter. Now . . .

I wondered whether the Pattern really held grudges. That is, how long would it be before it was safe to me to go forth without feeling in imminent peril? No real way to tell. Unfortunate. Still, the Pattern must have too much to occupy it to behave in any manner similar to those people who hung about in its vicinity—i.e., Amberites. Mustn't it? I took another drink. I might be here for a long time.

I would use a spell to alter my appearance, I decided. When I left here I would have dark hair and a beard (over the beginnings of a real beard), gray eyes, a straight nose, higher cheekbones, and a smaller chin. I would seem taller and a lot thinner. I would switch from my usual bright ones to dark garments. Not just some light, cosmetic spell either. It would have to be a strong one, with depth and substance to it.

Musing upon this, I got up and went in search of food. I found some tinned beef and biscuits, and I used a small spell to heat a can of soup. No, that was not a violation of the physical laws of the place. The crystal walls block sendings in and out, but my spells came in with me and operated as normal in the interior.

Eating, I thought again of Nayda, of Merlin, and of Coral. Whatever was happening to them—good or bad—time was favoring them in getting it done. Even if I stayed here for but a short while developments back home would be incommensurate with time's apparent lapse here. And what kind of time did the Pattern really keep? All of them, I supposed—that is to say, its own—but I also felt it to be especially keyed to the mainline of its flow in Amber. In fact, I was almost sure of it, since that's where the action was. So if I wanted to be back in action quickly I should just stay here long enough for my hand to heal.

But really, how badly could the Pattern want me? How much would I actually matter to it? What was I in its view? King of a minor Golden Circle realm. Assassin of one Prince of Amber. Son of the man who had once sought to destroy it . . . I winced at that, but reflected that the Pattern had let me live my entire life up to now without reprisal for dad's actions. And my part in the current business had been minimal. Coral had seemed its main concern, and then Merlin. Perhaps I was being ultra-cautious. Likely, it had dismissed me from its main considerations the moment I had vanished. Still, I wasn't going to step out of here without that disguise.

I finished eating and sipped at the wine. And when I did step out? What exactly would I be about then? Numerous possibilities tumbled through my mind. I also began yawning and the sleeping bag looked very good. Lightning flashed, blue wave through the walls. Then the thunder came, like surf. Tomorrow then. Tomorrow I would plan . . . I crawled inside and got comfortable. In a moment, I was gone.

I've no idea how long I slept. On rising, I made the rounds to establish a security habit, ran through a vigorous routine of exercises, cleaned myself up, then ate a leisurely breakfast. I felt better than I had the day before, and my hand had already commenced healing. Then I sat and stared at the wall, probably for hours. What was my best course of action?

I could rush back to Kashfa and the kingship, I could hunt after my friends, I could simply go underground, lie low, and investigate until I learned what was going on. It was a question of priorities. What was the most important thing I could do for everybody concerned? I thought about it till lunchtime and then I ate again.

Afterwards, I took up my small sketchpad and a pencil and I began recalling a certain lady, feature by feature. I fiddled with it all afternoon, to pass the time, though I knew I had her right. When I knocked off for dinner the next day's activities had already taken shape in my mind.

The next morning my injury was considerably diminished, and I conjured myself a mirror upon a smooth surface of the wall. Using an oil lamp so as not to waste an illumination spell, I conjured that tall, dark, lean figure upon my own form, cast those aquiline features upon my own—complete with beard—and I looked upon my work and saw that it was good. I transformed the appearance of my garments then, also, to keep the new me company—this latter a single spell. I'd have to fetch real garments as soon as I could. No use wasting a high-powered working on something that trivial. I did this all first thing, because I'd wanted to wear the guise all day, let it soak in, see whether there were any hidden weaknesses to my working. Then I wanted to sleep in it, for the same reason.

That afternoon I took up the sketchpad again. I studied my pervious day's work, then turned to a fresh page and executed a Trump. It felt exactly right. The next morning, following the usual routine, I reviewed myself in the mirror again, was satisfied, and mounted the ladder to emerge from the cave. It was a damp, cool morning with a few blue breaks in the cloud cover high overhead. Could rain again. But what the hell did I care? I was on my way out.

I reached for my pad, then paused. I was reminded of other Trumps I had dealt with over the years, and of something else. I withdrew my deck of cards. Uncasing them, I moved slowly through until I came to the sad one—dad's. I had kept his card for sentiment's sake, not utility. He looked just as I remembered him, but I hadn't sought it for purposes of reminiscence. It was because of the item he wore at his side.

I focused on Werewindle, by all accounts a magical blade, in some way related to Corwin's Greyswandir. And I recalled Merlin's telling me how his father had summoned Greyswandir to him in Shadow, following his escape from the dungeons of Amber. There was some special affinity between him and that weapon. I wondered. Now that the pace had quickened and new adventures were looming, it would probably be advisable to face things

Seven Tales in Amber

prepared with the appropriate steel. Though dad was dead, Werewindle was somehow alive. Though I could not reach my father, might I somehow reach his blade, its whereabouts, of last report, somewhere in the Courts of Chaos? I focused my attention upon it, calling it with my mind. It seemed that I felt something, and when I touched it the spot it occupied on the card seemed to be growing cold. I reached. Farther. harder.

And then there was clarity and nearness and the feeling of a cold, alien intelligence regarding me.

"Werewindle," I said softly.

If there can be the sound of an echo in the absence of a prior sound this is what I heard.

"Son of Brand," came a reverberation.

"Call me Luke." There was silence. Then, "Luke," came the vibration.

I reached forward, caught hold of it, and drew it toward me. The scabbard came with it. I drew back. I held it in my hands then and I drew it. It flowed like molten gold around the design it wore. I raised it, extended it, executed a cut. It felt right. It felt perfect. It felt as if enormous power lay behind its every movement.

"Thanks," I said, and the echo of laughter came and went.

I raised my pad and opened it to the appropriate page, hoping it was a good time to make the call. I regarded the lady's delicate features, her unfocused gaze that somehow indicated the breadth and depth of her vision. After a few moments, the page grew cold beneath my fingertips, and my drawing took on a 3-dimensional quality, seemed faintly to stir.

"Yes?" came her voice. "Your Highness." I said. "However you may perceive these things, I want you to know that I have intentionally altered my appearance. I was hoping that—"

"Luke," she said, "of course I recognize you—your own Majesty now," her gaze still unfocused. "You are troubled."

"Indeed I am." "You wish to come through?"

"If it is appropriate and convenient."

"Certainly."

She extended her hand. I reached forward, taking it lightly in my own, as her studio came clear, banishing gray skies and crystal hill, I took a step toward her and I was there. Immediately, I dropped to my knees, unclasped my swordbelt and offered her my blade. In the distance, I could hear sounds of hammering and sawing.

"Rise," she said, touching my shoulder. "Come and be seated. Have a cup of tea with me."

I got to my feet and followed her to a table in the corner. She took off her dusty apron and hung it on a peg on the wall. As she prepared the tea I regarded the small army of statues which lined one wall and bivouacked in random cluster about the enormous room—large, small, realistic, impressionistic, beautiful, grotesque. She worked mainly in clay, though a few smaller ones were of stone and there were furnaces at the room's far end, though these were cold now. Several metal mobiles of unusual shape were suspended from ceiling beams.

When she joined me again she reached out and touched my left hand, locating the ring she had given me.

"Yes, I value the Queen's protection," I said.

"Even though you are now a monarch yourself from a country on friendly terms with us?"

"Even so," I said. "So much so, in fact, that I wish to reciprocate in part."

"Oh?"

"I'm not at all certain that Amber is aware of recent events to which I have been party or of which I have knowledge, which may affect her welfare. That is, unless Merlin has been in touch recently."

"Merlin has not been in touch," she said. "If you have information vital to the realm, though, perhaps you ought to give it to Random direct. He's not here just now, but I could reach him for you via Trump."

"No," I said. "I know he doesn't like me at all or trust me, as his brother's killer and a friend of the man who has sworn to destroy Amber. I am sure he would love to see me deposed and some puppet on the throne of Kashfa. I suppose I must have things out with him one day, but this isn't the day. I've too much else going on just now. But the information transcends local politics. It involves Amber and the Courts of Chaos, the Pattern and the Logrus, the death of Swayvill and Merlin's possible succession to the throne in the Courts—"

"You're serious!"

"You bet. I know he'll listen to you. And he'll even understand why I told you. Let me avoid him this way. There are big events in the offing."

"Tell me," she said, raising her cup.

So I did, including everything Merlin had told me, up through the confrontation at the primal Pattern and my flight to the Crystal Cave. We went through the entire pot of tea in the process, and when I was finished we just sat for a time in silence.

Finally, she sighed.

"You have charged me to deliver major intelligence," she said.

"I know."

"Yet I feel it is but a small part of much greater developments."

"How's that?" I asked.

"A few small things I have heard, known, guessed at, and perhaps dreamed—and a few, I suppose, I simply fear. Hardly a coherent shape. Yet enough, perhaps, to query the powers of the earth I work with. Yes. Now that I have thought it I must try it, of course. At a time such as this."

She rose slowly, paused, and gestured high.

"That shall be the Tongue," she said, and a draft stirred one of the mobiles causing it to produce many tones.

She crossed the studio to the right hand wall—small figure in gray and green, chestnut hair down to the middle of her back—and ran her fingers lightly over the sculpted figure that stood there. Finally, selecting a broad-faced statue with a narrow torso, she began pushing it toward the center of the room. I was on my feet and moving in an instant.

"Let me do that for you, Your Highness."

She shook her head.

"Call me Vialle," she said. "And no, I must position them myself. This one is named Memory."

She placed it below and somewhat to the northwest of the Tongue. Then she moved to a knot of figures and selected a thin one with slightly parted lips, which she placed to the south on Tongue's compass.

"And this is Desire," she stated. Quickly locating a third—a tall, squinting figure—she placed it to the northeast.

"Caution," she went on.

A lady, her right hand boldly extended, went to the west.

"Risk," she continued.

To the east she positioned another lady, both arms spread wide.

"Heart," she said.

To the southwest went a high-domed, shaggy-browed philosopher. "Head," she said.

. . . And to the southeast a smiling lady—impossible to say whether her hand was raised in greeting or to deliver a blow.

"Chance," she finished, fitting her into the circle which had come to remind me both of Stonehenge and of Easter Island.

"Bring two chairs," she said, "and place them here and here."

She indicated positions to the north and south of her circle.

I did as she'd said, and she seated herself in the northern-most chair, behind a final figure she had placed: Foresight. I took my place back of Desire.

"Be silent now," she instructed

Then she sat still, hands in her lap, for several minutes.

Finally, "At the deepest level," she said, "what threatens the peace?"

From my left, Caution seemed to speak, though the Tongue chimed his words overhead.

"A redistribution of ancient powers," he said.

"In what manner?"

"That which was hidden becomes known and is moved about," answered Risk.

"Are both Amber and the Courts involved?"

"Indeed," answered Desire, from before me.

"Ancient powers," she said. "How ancient?"

"Before there was an Amber, they were," stated Memory.

"Before there was a Jewel of Judgement—the Eye of the Serpent?"

"No," Memory responded.

She drew a sudden breath.

"Their number?" she said.

"Eleven," Memory replied.

She grew pale at that, but I held my silence as she had instructed.

"Those responsible for this stirring of ashes," she said then, "what do they wish?"

"A return to the glory of days gone by," Desire stated.

"Could this end be realized?"

"Yes," Foresight replied.

"Could it be averted?"

"Yes," said Foresight.

"At peril," Caution added.

"How might one begin?"

"Query the guardians," Head stated.

"How bad is the situation?"

"It has already begun," Head answered.

"And the danger is already present," said Risk.

"So is opportunity," said Chance.

"Of what sort?" Vialle inquired.

There came a sound from across the room as my scabbard and blade slid to the floor from where I had leaned them against the wall. Vialle stared.

"My weapon," I said, "just slipped."

"Name it."

"It was my father's sword, called Werewindle."

"I know of it." Then, "This man, Luke," she said, "there is something about his blade and its sister weapon that figures in all of this. I do not know their stories, though."

"Yes, they are connected," said Memory.

"How?"

"They were created in a similar fashion at near to the same time, and they partake of the powers of which we have spoken," Memory replied.

"Will there be a conflict?"

"Yes," said Foresight.

"On what scale?"

Foresight was silent. Chance laughed.

"I do not understand."

"The laughter of Chance is uncertainty," Head responded.

"Will Luke figure in the conflict?"

"Yes," Foresight answered.

"Should he seek the guardians?"

"He must try," said Heart.

"And if he fails?"

"A Prince approaches even now who knows more of these matters," said Head.

"Who is that?"

"A prisoner freed," Head replied.

"Who?"

"He wears a silver rose," said Head. "He bears the other blade."

Vialle raised her head.

"Have you any questions?" she asked me.

"Yes. But I doubt I'd get an answer if I asked whether we'll win."

Chance laughed as Vialle rose.

She let me help move the statues back into place. Then, seated once more, I said to her, "'Seek the guardians?'"

"There is a custodian—possibly two," she replied. "A self-exiled Prince of Amber and his sister have guarded a portion of this power for a long while. It would seem in order to see that they still live, still discharge the duty."

"Self-exiled? Why?"

"Personal reasons, involving the late King."

Seven Tales in Amber

"Where are they?"

"I do not know."

"Then how could we find them?"

"There is a Trump."

She rose and moved to a small chest of drawers. Opening one, she withdrew a boxed set of cards.

Slowly, she counted dawn from the top of the deck and removed one.

When she returned she presented me with the card, portrait of a slim man with hair the color of rust.

"His name is Delwin," she said.

"You think I should just call him and ask whether he still has whatever he had?"

"State quickly that you are not of Amber," she told me, "but give your lineage. Ask whether his stewardship of the spikards remains intact. Try to find out where he is, or to go through and discuss it face to face if you can."

"Right," I said, not wanting to tell her that I had spoken—very briefly—with him before in seeking allies in my war against Amber. He'd dismissed me out of hand, but I didn't want to stir Vialle's memories of those days. So I simply said, "Okay. I'll give it a try."

I decided to fast-talk him at first, to give him time to think, to realize that I was not alone, and not to let slip anything of our earlier exchange. My altered appearance should help in this, too.

I reached for contact.

First, the coldness, then a feeling of personality suddenly alert.

"Who is it?" I felt the question even before the likeness took on depth and life.

"Luke Reynard, otherwise known as Rinaldo," I answered, as the card was suddenly animated and I felt his scrutiny, "King of Kashfa and B.S. in Business Management, University of California at Berkeley." Our gazes locked. He seemed neither belligerent nor friendly. "I wanted to know whether your stewardship of the spikards remains intact."

"Luke-Rinaldo," he said, "just what is your concern in this, and how did you come to learn of the matter?"

"While I am not of Amber," I replied, "my father was. I know it is soon to become a matter of concern in that place because of Merlin—son of Corwin—apparently being in direct line for the succession to the throne in the Courts of Chaos."

"I know who Merlin is," Delwin sated. "Who is your father?"

"Prince Brand."

"And your mother?"

"The Lady Jasra, formerly Queen of Kashfa. Now, might we talk about this matter a little?"

"No," Delwin said. "We may not."

He moved his hand as if to break the contact.

"Wait!" I said. "Do you have a microwave oven?"

He hesitated.

"A what?"

"It's a box-like device that can warm a meal in a matter of minutes. I've worked out a general spell to allow one to operate in most of Shadow. Wake up in the middle of the night with a taste for a steaming hot tuna casserole? Take one out of the freezer, unwrap it, and pop it in. What's a freezer? Glad you asked. It's another box, with eternal winter inside. Store meals in there, take one out and zap it in the mike whenever the fancy hits. And yes, I can supply the freezer, too. You don't want to talk spikards, let's talk business. I can give you a deal on these devices, in quantity, that will meet or beat the price of anyone else capable of supplying them—and I don't think it would be an easy thing to find another supplier. But that's not all I can do for you—"

"I'm sorry," said Delwin. "No solicitors either." His hand moved again.

"Wait!" I cried. "I'll make you an offer you can't refuse!"

He broke the connection.

"Come back," I willed after his image, but it went 2-dimensional and warmed to room temperature again.

"Sorry," I said to Vialle. "I gave it my best shot, but he wasn't buying any."

"To tell the truth, I didn't think you'd hold him even that long. But I could tell he was interested in you until you mentioned your mother. Then something changed."

"Wouldn't be the first time," I said. "I've a mind to try him again later."

"In that case, keep the Trump."

"I don't need it, Vialle. I'll make my own when the time comes."

"You are an artist and a Trump master?"

"Well, I do paint. Fairly seriously sometimes."

"Then you must see all of my works while you wait. I'd value your opinion."

"My pleasure," I said. 'You mean while I wait—"

"—for Corwin."

"Ah, just so. Thank you."

"You can be the first to use one of the new rooms. We've been doing a lot of reconstruction and remodeling since the Logrus and the Pattern had their confrontation."

"I heard about it," I said. "Very well. I wonder when he'll arrive?"

"Soon, I feel," she said. "I'll summon a servant to get you settled now. Another will bring you to dine with me later, and we can discuss art."

"That will be fine."

Blue Horse, Dancing Mountains

I took a right at the Burning Wells and fled smokeghosts across the Uplands of Artine. I slew the leader of the Kerts of Shern as her flock harried me from high towered perches among the canyons of that place. The others abandoned the sport, and we were through, beneath a green rain out of a slate-colored sky. Onward and down then, to where the plains swirled dust devils that sang of sad eternities in rock that once they were.

At last the winds fell off and Shask, my deadly mount, blue stallion out of Chaos, slowed to a stop before vermilion sands.

"What is the matter?" I asked.

"We must cross this neck of the desert to reach the Dancing Mountains," Shask replied.

"And how long a journey might that be?"

"Most of the rest of the day," he said. "It is narrowest here. We have paid in part for this indulgence already. The rest will come in the mountains themselves, for now we must cross where they are very active."

I raised my canteen and shook it.

"Worth it," I said, "so long as they don't really dance in Richter terms."

"No, but at the Great Divide between the shadows of Amber and the shadows of Chaos there is some natural shifting activity in play where they meet."

"I'm no stranger to shadow-storms, which is what that sounds like—a permanent shadow-storm front. But I wish we could just push on through rather than camp there."

"I told you when you chose me, Lord Corwin, that I could bear you farther than any other mount by day. But by night I become an unmoving serpent, hardening to stone and cold as a demon's heart, thawing come dawn."

"Yes, I recall," I said, "and you have served me well, as Merlin said you might. Perhaps we should overnight this side of the mountains and cross tomorrow."

Seven Tales in Amber

"The front, as I said, shifts. Likely, at some point, it would join you in the foothills or before. Once you reach the region, it matters not where we spend the night. The shadows will dance over us or near us. Dismount now, please, unsaddle, and remove your gear, that I may shift."

"To what?" I asked as I swung to the ground.

"I've a lizard form would face this desert best."

"By all means, Shask, be comfortable, be efficient. Be a lizard."

I set about unburdening him. It was good to be free again.

Shask as blue lizard was enormously fast and virtually tireless. He got us across the sands with daylight to spare, and as I stood beside him contemplating the trail that led upward through the foothills, he spoke in a sibilant tone: "As I said, the shadows can catch us anywhere around here, and I still have strength to take us up for an hour or so before we camp, rest, and feed. What is your choice?"

"Go," I told him.

Trees changed their foliage even as I watched. The trail was maddeningly irregular, shifting its course, changing its character beneath us. Seasons came and went—a flurrying of snow followed by a blast of hot air, then springtime and blooming flowers. There were glimpses of towers and metal people, highways, bridges, tunnels gone in moments. Then the entire dance would shift away and we would simply be mounting a trail again.

At last, we made camp in a sheltered area near to a summit. Clouds collected as we ate, and a few rumbles under rolled in the distance. I made myself a low lean-to. Shask transformed himself into a great dragonheaded, winged, feathered serpent, and coiled nearby.

"A good night to you, Shask," I called out, as the first drops fell.

"And-to-you-Corwin," he said softly.

I lay back, closed my eyes, and was asleep almost immediately. How long I slept, I do not know. I was jarred out of it, however, by a terrific clap of thunder which seemed to occur directly overhead.

I found myself sitting up, having reached out to and half drawn Grayswandir, before the echoes died. I shook my head and sat listening.

Something seemed to be missing and I could not determine what.

There came a brilliant flash of light and another thunderclap. I flinched at them and sat waiting for more, but only silence followed.

Silence . . .

I stuck my hand outside the lean-to, then my head. It had stopped raining. That was the missing item—the splatter of droplets.

My gaze was attracted by a glow from beyond the nearby summit. I pulled on my boots and departed the shelter. Outside, I buckled on my sword belt and fastened my cloak at the neck. I had to investigate. In a place like this, any activity might represent a threat.

I touched Shask—who indeed felt stony—as I passed, and made my way to where the trail had been. It was still there, though diminished in width, and I set foot upon it and climbed upward. The light source for which I was headed seemed to be moving slightly. Now, faintly, in the distance, I seemed to hear the sound of rainfall. Perhaps it was coming down on the other side of the peak.

As I advanced, I became convinced that it was storming not too far away. I could now hear the moaning of wind within the splashing.

I was suddenly dazzled by a flash from beyond the crest. A sharp report of thunder kept it company. I halted for only a moment. During that time, amid the ringing in my ears, I thought that I heard the sound of a cackling laugh.

Trudging ahead, I came at last to the summit. Immediately, the wind assailed me, bearing a full load of moisture. I drew my cloak closed and fastened it down the front as I made my way forward.

Several paces then, and I beheld a hollow, below and to my left. It was eerily illuminated by dancing orbs of ball lightning. There were two figures within it—one seated on the ground, the other, cross-legged, hanging upside down in the air with no apparent means of support, across from him. I chose the most concealed route I could and headed toward them.

They were lost to my sight much of the way, as the course I had taken bore me through areas of fairly dense foliage. Abruptly, however, I knew that I was near when the rain ceased to fall upon me and I no longer felt the pressures of the wind. It was as if I had entered the still eye of a hurricane.

Cautiously, I continued my advance, winding up on my belly, peering amid branches at the two old men. Both regarded the invisible cubes of a three-dimensional game, pieces hung above a board on the ground between them, squares of their aerial positions limned faintly in fire. The man seated upon the ground was a hunchback, and he was smiling, and I knew him. It was Dworkin Barimen, my legendary ancestor, filled with ages and wisdom and godlike powers, creator of Amber, the Pattern, the Trumps, and maybe reality itself as I understood it. Unfortunately, through much of my dealing with him in recent times, he'd also been more than a little bit nuts.

Merlin had assured me that he was recovered now, but I wondered. Godlike beings are often noted for some measure of nontraditional rationality. It just seems to go with the territory. I wouldn't put it past the old bugger to be using sanity as a pose while in pursuit of some paradoxical end.

The other man, whose back was to me, reached forward and moved a piece that seemed to correspond to a pawn. It was a representation of the Chaos beast known as a Fire Angel. When the move was completed the lightning flashed again and the thunder cracked and my body tingled. Then Dworkin reached out and moved one of his pieces, a Wyvern. Again, the thunder and lightning, the tingling. I saw that a rearing Unicorn occupied the place of the King among Dworkin's pieces, a representation of the palace at Amber on the square beside it. His opponent's King an erect Serpent, the Thelbane—the great needle-like palace of the Kings of Chaos—beside it.

Dworkin's opponent advanced a Piece, laughing as he did so. "Mandor," he announced. "He thinks himself puppet-master and king-maker." After the crash and dazzle, Dworkin moved a piece. "Corwin," he said.

"He is free again."

"Yes. But he does not know he is in a race with destiny. I doubt he will make it back to Amber in time to encounter the hall of mirrors. Without their clues, how effective will he be?"

Dworkin smiled and raised his eyes. For a moment, he seemed to be looking right at me. "I think his timing is perfect, Suhuy," he said then, "and I have several pieces of his memory I found years ago drifting above the Pattern in Rebma. I wish I had a golden piss-pot for each time he's been underestimated."

"What would that give you?" asked the other.

"Expensive helmets for his enemies."

Both men laughed, and Suhuy rotated 90 degrees counterclockwise. Dworkin rose into the air and tilted forward until he was parallel to the ground, looking down on the board. Suhuy tended a hand toward a female figure on one of the higher levels, then drew it back. Abruptly, he moved the Fire Angel again. Even as the air was burned and beaten Dworkin made a move, so that the thunder continued into a roll and the brightness hung there. Dworkin said something I could not hear over the din. Suhuy's response to the probable naming was, "But she's a Chaos figure!"

"So? We set no rule against it. Your move."

"I want to study this," Suhuy said. "More than a little."

"Take it with you," Dworkin responded. "Bring it back tomorrow night?"

"I'll be occupied. The night after?"

"I will be occupied. Three nights hence?"

"Yes. Until then—"

"—good night."

The blast and the crash that followed blinded me and deafened me for several moments. Suddenly, I felt the rain and the wind. When my vision cleared, I saw that the hollow was empty. Retreating, I made my way back over the crest and down to my camp, which the rain had found again, also. The trail was wider now.

I rose at dawn and fed myself while I waited for Shask to stir. The night's doings did not seem like a dream.

"Shask," I said later, "do you know what a hellride is?"

"I've heard of it," he replied, "as an arcane means of traveling great distances in a short time, employed by the House of Amber. Said to be hazardous to the mental health of the noble steed."

"You strike me as being eminently stable, emotionally and intellectually."

"Why, thank you—I guess. Why the sudden rush?"

"You slept through a great show," I said, "and now I've a date with a gang of reflections if I can catch them before they fade."

"If it must be done . . ."

"We race for the golden piss-pot, my friend. Rise up and be a horse."

The Shroudling and the Guisel

I awoke in a dark room, making love to a lady I did not recall having gone to bed with. Life can be strange. Also oddly sweet at times. I hadn't the will to destroy our congress, and I went on and on with what I was doing and so did she until we came to that point of sudden giving and taking, that moment of balance and rest.

I made a gesture with my left hand and a small light appeared and glowed above our heads. She had long black hair and green eyes, and her cheekbones were high and her brow wide. She laughed when the light came on, revealing the teeth of a vampire. Her mouth held not a trace of blood, making it seem somehow impolite for me to touch my throat seeking after any trace of soreness. "It's been a long time, Merlin," she said softly.

"Madam, you have the advantage of me," I said.

She laughed again. "Hardly," she answered, and she moved in such a fashion as to distract me entirely, causing the entire chain of events to begin again on my part.

"Unfair," I said, staring into those sea-deep eyes, stroking that pale brow. There was something terribly familiar there, but I could not understand it.

"Think," she said, "for I wish to be remembered."

"I . . . Rhanda?" I asked.

"Your first love, as you were mine," she said smiling, "there in the mausoleum. Children at play, really. But it was sweet, was it not?"

"It still is," I replied, stroking her hair. "No, I never forgot you. Never thought to see you again, though, after finding that note saying your parents no longer permitted you to play with me . . . thinking me a vampire."

"It seemed so, my Prince of Chaos and of Amber. Your strange strengths and your magics . . . . ."

I looked at her mouth, at her unsheathed fangs. "Odd thing for a family of vampires to forbid," I stated.

"Vampires? We're not vampires," she said. "We are among the last of the

43

shroudlings. There are only five families of us left in all the secret images of all the shadows from here to Amber—and farther, on into that place and into Chaos."

I held her more tightly and a long lifetime of strange lore passed through my head. Later I said, "Sorry, but I have no idea of what a shroudling is."

Later still she responded, "I would be very surprised if you did, for we have always been a secret race." She opened her mouth to me, and I saw by spirit-light a slow retraction of her fangs into normal-seeming dentition. "They emerge in times of passion other than feasting," she remarked.

"So you do use them as a vampire would," I said.

"Or a ghoul," she said. "Their flesh is even richer than their blood."

"'Their'?" I said.

"That of those we would take."

"And who might they be?" I asked.

"Those the world might be better off without," she said. "Most of them simply vanish. Occasionally, with a feast of jokers, only parts of some remain."

I shook my head.

"Shroudling lady, I do not understand," I told her.

"We come and go where we would. We are an undetected people, a proud people. We live by a code of honor which has protected us against all your understanding. Even those who suspect us do not know where to turn to seek us."

"Yet you come and tell me these things."

"I have watched you much of my life. You would not betray us. You, too, live by a code."

"Watched me much of my life? How?"

But we distracted each other then and that moment came to a close. I would not let it die, however. Finally, as we lay side by side, I repeated it. By then, however, she was ready for it.

"I am the fleeting shadow in your mirror," she said. "I look out, yet you see me not. All of us have our pets, my love, a person or place of hobby. You have always been mine."

"Why do you come to me now, Rhanda?" I asked. "After all these years?"

She looked away.

"Mayhap you will die soon," she said after a time, "and I wished to recall our happy days together at Wildwood."

"Die soon? I live in danger. I can't deny it. I'm too near the Throne. But I've strong protectors—and I am stronger than people think."

"As I said, I have watched," she stated. "I do not doubt your prowess. I've seen you hang many spells and maintain them. Some of them I do not even understand."

"You are a sorceress?"

She shook her head. "My knowledge of these matters, while extensive, is purely academic," she said. "My own powers lie elsewhere."

"Where?" I inquired.

She gestured toward my wall. I stared. Finally, I said, "I don't understand."

"Could you turn that thing up?" she asked, nodding toward the spirit-light. I did so.

"Now move it into the vicinity of your mirror."

I did that also. The mirror was very dark, but so was everything else there in Mandor's guest house, where I had elected to spend the night following our recent reconciliation.

I got out of bed and crossed the room. The mirror was absolutely black, containing no reflection of anything. "Peculiar," I remarked.

"No," she said. "I closed it and locked it after I entered here. Likewise, every other mirror in the house."

"You came in by way of the mirror?"

"I did. I live in the mirrorworld."

"And your family? And the four other families you mentioned?"

"We all of us make our homes beyond the bounds of reflection."

"And from there you travel from place to place?"

"Indeed."

"Obviously, to watch your pets. And to eat people of whom you disapprove?"

"That, too."

"You're scary, Rhanda." I returned to the bed, seating myself on its edge. I took hold of her hand and held it. "And it is good to see you again. I wish you had come to me sooner."

"I have," she said, "using the sleep spells of our kind."

"I wish you had awakened me."

She nodded. "I would like to have stayed with you, or taken you home with me. But for this part of your life you a certified danger bringer."

"It does seem that way," I agreed. "Still . . . Why are you here now, apart from the obvious?"

"The danger has spread. It involves us now."

"I actually thought that the danger in my life had been minimized a bit of late," I told her. "I have beaten off Dara's and Mandor's attempts to control me and come to an understanding of sorts with them."

"Yet still they will scheme."

I shrugged. "It is their nature. They know that I know, and they know I am their match. They know I am ready for them now. And my brother Jurt . . . we, too, seem to have reached an understanding. And Julia . . . we have been reconciled. We—"

She laughed. "Julia has already used your 'reconciliation' to try to turn Jurt against you. I watched. I know. She stirs his jealousy with hints that she still cares more for you than for him. What she really wants is you removed, along with the seven in the running with you—and the others who stand ready. She would be queen in Chaos."

"She's no match for Dara," I said.

"Ever since she defeated Jasra, she's had a high opinion of herself. It has not occurred to her that Jasra had grown lazy and lost by a trick, not by a matter of power. She would rather believe her own strength greater than it is. And that is her weakness. She would be reunited with you to put you off-guard as well as to turn your brother against you once again."

"I am forewarned, and I thank you—though there are really only six others in the running for the Throne. I was number one, but a half dozen pretenders have recently turned up. You said seven. There's one I don't know about?"

"There is the hidden one," she said. "I do not know his name to tell you, though I know you saw him in Suhuy's pool. I know his appearance, Chaotic and human. I know that even Mandor considers him a worthy antagonist when it comes to scheming. Conversely, I believe Mandor is the main reason he removed himself to our realm. He fears Mandor."

"He inhabits the mirrorworld?"

"Yes, though he is not yet aware of our existence there. He found it by a near-impossible accident, but he simply thinks he has made a marvelous discovery—a secret way to go nearly anywhere, to see nearly anything without detection. Our people have avoided his awareness, using curves he cannot perceive let alone turn. It has made him considerably more formidable in his path to the Throne."

"If he can look out—even listen—through any mirror without being detected; if he can step out; assassinate someone, and escape by the same route—yes, I can understand it."

The night suddenly seemed very cold. Rhanda's eyes widened. I moved to the chair where I had thrown my garments and began dressing myself.

"Yes, do that," she said.

"There's more, isn't there?"

"Yes. The hidden one has located and brought back an abomination to our peaceful realm. Somewhere, he found a guisel."

"What is a guisel?"

"A being out of our myth, one we had thought long exterminated in the mirrorworld. Its kind nearly destroyed the shroudlings. A monster, it took an entire family to destroy what was thought to be the last of them."

I buckled my sword belt and drew on my boots. I crossed the chamber to the mirror and held my hand before its blackness. Yes, it seemed the source of the cold.

"You closed them and locked them?" I said. "All of the mirrors in this vicinity?"

"The hidden one has sent the guisel through the ways of the mirrors to destroy nine rivals to the Throne. It is on its way to seek the tenth now: yourself."

"I see. Can it break your locks?"

"I don't know. Not easily, I wouldn't think. It brings the cold, however. It lurks just beyond the mirror. It knows that you are here."

"What does it look like?"

"A winged eel with a multitude of clawed legs. It is about 10 feet long."

"If we let it in?"

"It will attack you."

"If we enter the mirror ourselves?"

"It will attack you."

"On which side is it stronger?"

"The same on either, I think."

"Well, hell! Can we enter by a different mirror and sneak up on it?"

"Maybe."

"Let's give it a shot. Come on."

*

She rose, dressed quickly in a blood-red garment, and followed me through a wall to a room that was actually several miles distant. Like most of the nobles of Chaos, brother Mandor believes in keeping a residence scattered. A long mirror hung on the far wall between the desk and a large Chaos clock. The clock, I saw, was about to chime a nonlinear for the observer. Great. I drew my blade.

"I didn't even know this one was here," she said.

"We're some distance away from the room where I slept. Forget space. Take me through."

"I'd better warn you first," she said. "According to tradition, nobody's ever succeeded in killing a guisel with a sword, or purely by means of magic. Guisels can absorb spells and lashes of force. They can take terrible wounds and survive."

"Any suggestions then?"

"Baffle it, imprison it, banish it. That might be better than trying to kill it."

"OK, we'll play it as it's dealt. If I get into real bad trouble, you get the hell out."

She did not reply but took my hand and stepped into the mirror. As I followed her, the antique Chaos clock began to chime an irregular beat. The inside of the mirror seemed the same as the room without, but turned around. Rhanda led me to the farthest point of the reflection, to the left, then stepped around a corner.

We came into a twisted, twilit place of towers and great residences, none of them familiar to me. The air bore clusters of wavy, crooked lines here and there. She approached one, inserted her free hand, and stepped through it, taking me with her. We emerged on a crooked street lined with twisted buildings.

"Thank you," I said then, "for the warning and for the chance to strike."

She squeezed my hand.

"It is not just for you, but for my family, also, that I do it."

"I know that," I said.

"I would not be doing this if I did not believe that you have a chance against the thing. If I did not, I would simply have warned you and told you what I know. But I also remember one day . . . back in Wildwood . . . when you promised to be my champion. You seemed a real hero to me then."

I smiled as I recalled that gloomy day. We had been reading tales of chivalry in the mausoleum. In a fit of nobility I led her outside as the thunder rolled, and I stood among the grave markers of unknown mortals—Dennis Colt, Remo Williams, John Gaunt—and swore to be her champion if ever she needed one. She had kissed me then, and I had hoped for some immediate evil circumstance against which to pit myself on her behalf. But none occurred.

We moved ahead, and she counted doors, halting at the seventh. "That one," she said, "leads through the curves to the place behind the locked mirror in your room."

Seven Tales in Amber

I released her hand and moved past her.

"All right," I said, "time to go a-guiseling," and I advanced. The guisel saved me the trouble of testing the curves by emerging before I got there.

Ten or 12 feet in length, it was, and eyeless as near as I could tell, with rapid-beating cilia all over what I took to be its head. It was very pink, with a long, green stripe passing about its body in one direction, and a blue one in the other. It raised its cilia-end three or four feet above the ground and swayed. It made a squeaking sound. It turned in my direction. Underneath it had a large, angled mouth like that of a shark; it opened and closed it several times and I saw many teeth. A green, venomous-seeming liquid dripped from that orifice to steam upon the ground.

I waited for it to come to me, and it did. I studied the way it moved—quickly, as it turned out—on the horde of small legs. I held my blade before me in an *en garde* position as I awaited its attack. I reviewed my spells.

It came on, and I hit it with my Runaway Buick and my Blazing Outhouse spells. In each instance, it stopped dead and waited for the spell to run its course. The air grew frigid and steamed about its mouth and midsection. It was as if it were digesting the magic and rushing it down entropy lane. When the steaming stopped, it advanced again and I hit it with my Demented Power Tools spell. Again, it halted, remained motionless, and steamed. This time I rushed forward and struck it a great blow with my blade. It rang like a bell, but nothing else happened, and I drew back as it stirred.

"It seems to eat my spells and excrete refrigeration," I said.

"This has been noted by others," Rhanda responded.

Even as we spoke, it torqued its body, moving that awful mouth to the top, and it lunged at me. I thrust my blade down its throat as its long legs clawed at or caught hold of me. I was driven over backwards as it closed its mouth, and I heard a shattering sound. I was left holding only a hilt. It had bitten off my blade. Frightened, I felt after my new power as the mouth opened again.

The gates of the spikard were opened, and I struck the creature with a raw force from somewhere in Shadow. Again, the thing seemed frozen as the air about me grew chill. I tore myself away from it, bleeding from dozens of small wounds. I rolled away and rose to my feet, still lashing it with the spikard, holding it cold. I tried using the blade to dismember it, but all it did was eat the attack and remain a statue of pink ice.

Reaching out through Shadow, I found myself another blade. With its tip, I traced a rectangle in the air, a bright circle at its center. I reached into it with my will and desire. After a moment, I felt contact.

"Dad! I feel you but I can't see you!"

"Ghostwheel," I said, "I am fighting for my life, and doubtless those of many others. Come to me if you can."

"I am trying. But you have found your way into a strange space. I seem to be barred from entering there."

"Damn!"

"I agree. I have faced this problem before in my travels. It does not lend itself to ready resolution."

The guisel began to move again. I tried to maintain the Trump contact but it was fading. "Father!" Ghostwheel cried as I lost hold. "Try—" Then he was gone. I backed away. I glanced at Rhanda. Dozens of other shroudlings now stood with her, all of them wearing black, white, or red garments. They began to sing a strange, dirgelike song, as if a dark soundtrack were required for our struggle. It did seem to slow the guisel, and it reminded me of something from long ago.

I threw back my head and gave voice to that ululant cry I had heard once in a dream and never forgotten.

My friend came.

Kergma—the living equation—came sliding in from many angles at once. I watched and waited as he/she/it—I had never been certain—assembled itself. Kergma had been a childhood playmate, along with Glait and Gryll.

Rhanda must have remembered the being who could go anywhere, for I heard her gasp. Kergma passed around and around her body in greeting, then came to me and did the same.

"My friends! It has been so long since you called me to play! I have missed you!"

51

Seven Tales in Amber

The guisel dragged itself forward against the song of the shroudlings as if beginning to overcome its power. "This is not a game," I answered. "That beast will destroy us all unless we nail it first," I said.

"*Then I must solve it for us. Everything that lives is an equation, a complex quantum study. I told you that long ago.*"

"Yes. Try. Please."

I feared blasting the thing again with the spikard while Kergma worked on it, lest it interfere with his calculations. I kept my blade and spikard at ready as I continued to back away. The shroudlings retreated with me, slowly.

"*A deadly balance,*" Kergma said at last. "*It has a wonderful life equation. Use your toy to stop it now.*"

I froze it again with the spikard. The shroudlings' song went on.

At length Kergma said,"*There is a weapon that can destroy it under the right circumstances. You must reach for it, however. It is a twisted blade you have wielded before. It hangs on the wall of a bar where once you drank with Luke.*"

"The Vorpal Sword?" I said. "It can kill it?"

"*A piece at a time, under the proper circumstances.*"

"You know these circumstances?"

"*I have solved for them.*"

I clutched my weapon and struck the guisel again with a force from the spikard. It squeaked and grew still. Then I discarded the blade I held and reached—far, far out through Shadow. I was a long time in finding what I sought and I had a resistance to overcome, so I added the force of the spikard to my own and it came to me. Once again, I held the shining, twisted Vorpal Sword in my hands.

I moved to strike at the guisel with it, but Kergma stopped me. So I hit it again with a lash of force from the spikard.

"*Not the way. Not the way.*"

"What then?"

"*We require a Dyson variation on the mirror equation.*"

"Show me."

Walls of mirrors shot up on all sides about me, the guisel, and Kergma, but

52

excluding Rhanda. We rose into the air and drifted toward the center of the sphere. Our reflections came at us from everywhere.

"*Now. But you must keep it from touching the walls.*"

"Save your equation. I may want to do something with it by and by."

I struck the dormant guisel with the Vorpal Sword. Again, it emitted a bell-like tone and remained quiescent.

"No," Kergma said. "*Let it thaw.*"

So I waited until it began to stir, meaning that it would be able to attack me soon. Nothing is ever easy. From outside, I still heard the faint sounds of singing.

The guisel recovered more quickly than I had anticipated. But I swung and lopped off half its head, which seemed to divide itself into tissue—thin images which then flew away in every direction.

"Caloo! Callay!" I cried, swinging again and removing a long section of tissue from its right side, which repeated the phenomenon of the ghosting and the flight. It came on again and I cut again. Another chunk departed from its twisting body in the same fashion. Whenever its writhing took it near a wall, I intervened with my body and sword, driving it back toward the center and hacking at or slicing it.

Again and again it came on or flipped toward the wall. Each time my response was similar. But it did not die. I fought it til but a tip of its writhing tail moved before me.

"Kergma," I said then, "we've sent most of it down infinite lines. Now, can you revise the equation? Then I'll find sufficient mass with the spikard to allow you to create another guisel for me—one that will return to the sender of this one and regard that person as prey."

"*I think so,*" Kergma said. "*I take it you left that final piece for the new one to eat?*"

"Yes, that was my thinking."

And so it was done. When the walls came down, the new guisel—black, its stripes red and yellow—was rubbing against my ankles like a cat. The singing stopped.

Seven Tales in Amber

"Go and seek the hidden one," I said, "and return the message."

It raced off, passing a curve and vanishing.

"What have you done?" Rhanda asked me. So I told her.

"The hidden one will now consider you the most dangerous of his rivals," she said, "if he lives. Probably he will increase his efforts against you, in subtlety as well as violence."

"Good," I said. "That is my hope. I'd like to force a confrontation. He will probably not feel safe in your world now either, never knowing when a new guisel might come a-hunting."

"True," she said. "You have been my champion," and she kissed me.

Just then, out of nowhere, a paw appeared and fell upon the blade I held. Its opposite waved two slips of paper before me. Then a soft voice spoke: "You keep borrowing that sword without signing for it. Kindly do that now, Merlin. The other slip is for last time." I found a ballpoint beneath my cloak and signed as the rest of the cat materialized. "That'll be $40," it said then. "It costs 20 bucks for each hour or portion of an hour, to vorp."

I dug around in my pockets and came up with the fees. The cat grinned and began to fade. "Good doing business with you," it said through the smile. "Come back soon. The next drink's on the house. And bring Luke. He's a great baritone."

I noticed as it faded that the shroudling family had also vanished.

Kregma moved nearer. "*Where are the others—Glait and Gryll?*"

"I left Grait in a wood," I replied, "though he may well be back in the Windmaster's vase in Gramble's museum in the Ways of Sawall by now. If you see him, tell him that the bigger thing has not eaten me—and he will drink warm milk with me one night and hear more tales yet. Gryll, I believe, is in the employ of my Uncle Suhuy."

"*Ah, the Windmaster . . . those were the days,*" he said. "*Yes, we must get together and play again. Thank you for calling me for this one,*" and he slid off in many directions and was gone, like the others.

"What now?" Rhanda asked.

"I am going home and back to bed." I hesitated, then said, "Come with me?"

She hesitated too, then nodded. "Let us finish the night as we began it," she said.

We walked through the seventh door and she unlocked my mirror. I knew that she would be gone when I awoke.

Coming to a Cord

It is no fun being tied to a bedpost when you are feeling under the weather. I phased back and forth between visibility and invisibility uncontrollably. On the other wrist, I felt my ability to communicate beginning to return. My increased sentience had remained with me ever since my strange journey with Merlin in the place between shadows. But there was a shock on my return to this reality. Slowly now, I was recovering from it, though some of the symptoms were slower in going than others. Consequently, it took me much longer than it normally would have to unknot myself.

I am Frakir, strangling cord to Merlin—Lord of Amber and Prince of Chaos. Normally, too, he would never have abandoned me like this, in the blasted apartments of Brand, late Prince of Amber and would-be Lord of the Universe. But he was under a mild spell Brand had actually left about for his son Rinaldo. However, Merlin has such a strong affinity with Rinaldo—also known as Luke—by virtue of their long association, that the spell latched onto him. He must have shaken it by now, but that still left me in an awkward position, with him doubtless back in the Courts.

I did not feel like waiting around with all the rebuilding and redecorating going on. They could decide to chuck the bed, with me attached, and go for all new stuff.

I finished unknotting myself. At least Merlin had used no magic when he'd tied me there. On the other hand, it was a tight knot, and I squirmed for a long while to get myself unlooped. Finally, the thing was loosened and I was able to undo it. Once I had freed myself from its subtle geometries, I slithered down the bedpost to the ground. This left me in a position to slip away, should a gang of furniture movers suddenly appear. In fact, it suddenly seemed a good idea to get out of the fast traffic lane now.

I moved away from the bed—out of Brand's room and into Merlin's—wondering what had been the secret of that ring he'd found and

57

put on—the spikard thing.

That it was extremely powerful and drew its energies from many sources was obvious to a being such as myself. That it seemed a thing of the same order as the sword Werewindle was also readily apparent, despite their varied forms to the eye of a human. Suddenly, it occurred to me that Merlin might not notice this, and I began to think that it might be necessary he should.

I crossed his room. I can move like a snake when I would. I have no ability to transport myself magically like almost everyone else I know, so I figured it were best to find someone who did. My only problem was that, in keeping with the family's general policy of personal secrecy on everything from magic to souffle recipes, many of them did not even know I existed.

. . . And for that matter I didn't know the location of their apartments, save for Merlin's, Brand's, Random and Vialle's, and Martin's—which Merlin sometimes visited. Random and Vialle's would be hard to reach, with all the work that was going on. So I headed off in the direction of Martin's rooms and slithered under the door when I got there. He had rock posters on most of his walls, as well as the speakers for a magically powered CD player. He, alas, was absent, and I had no idea when he might return.

I went back out into the hall and slithered along it, listening for a familiar voice, checking under doors, into rooms. This went on for some time before I heard Flora say, "Oh, bother!" from behind a door up the hall. I headed in that direction. She was one of the ones privy to my existence.

Her door was closed, but I was able to make my way beneath it into a highly decorated sitting room. She seemed in the process of mending a broken fingernail with some sort of goo.

I crossed the room to her side, maintaining my invisibility, and wrapped myself about her right ankle.

Hello, I said. *This is Frakir, Merlin's friend and strangling cord. Can you help me?*

Following a moment of silence, she said, "Frakir! What's happened? What do you need?"

I was inadvertently abandoned, I explained, while Merlin was under the influence of a peculiar spell. I need to get in touch with him. I've realized something he may need to know. Also, I want to get back on his wrist.

"I'll give his Trump a try," she said, "though if he's in the Courts I'll probably not be able to reach him."

I heard her open a drawer, and moments later I listened to her fumbling with cards. I tried to tune in on her thoughts as she manipulated them, but I could not.

"Sorry," she said, after a time. "I can't seem to get through to him."

Thanks for trying, I told her.

"When did you get separated from Merlin?" she asked.

It was the day the Powers met in the back hall, I said.

"What sort of spell did Merlin get caught up in?"

One that was hanging fairly free in Brand's quarters. You see, Merlin's and Brand's rooms being next door to each other, he'd entered out of curiosity when the wall fell during the confrontation.

"Frakir, I don't think that was an accident," she said. "One Power or the other probably arranged for things to be so."

Seems likely when one thinks about it, Princess.

"What do you want to do now? I'll be glad to help," she said.

I'd like to find a way to get back to Merlin, I said. He's had a general aura of danger about him for some time—to which I am particularly sensitive.

"I understand," she said, "and I'll find a way. It may take a few days, but I'll figure something."

All right. I'll wait, I said. I've no real choice in the matter.

"You're welcome to stay with me till that happens."

I'll do that, I said. Thanks.

I found a comfortable-looking table and wrapped myself about one of its legs. I went into stasis then, if one needs a word for it. It is not sleep, as there is no loss of consciousness. But there is no thinking in the conventional sense either. I just sort of spread out my awareness and am, until I am needed.

How long I lay coiled in this position, I have no way of telling. I was alone in the sitting room, though I was aware of Flora's breathing next door.

Seven Tales in Amber

Suddenly, she shrieked. This time, I just loosened myself and dropped to the floor.

As I began hurrying toward the room I heard another voice. "Sorry," it said. "I am pursued. I had no choice but to drop in without invitation."

"Who are you?" she asked.

"Well, I'm a sorcerer," he said. "I was hiding in your mirror, as I have every night for a long while. I have this crush on you and I like to watch you as you go about your business."

"Peeping Tom—a voyeur!" she said.

"No," he said. "I think you're a really nice-looking lady, and I like watching you. That's all."

"There are many legitimate ways by which you could have gained an introduction," she said.

"True, but that way might have led to horrible complications in my life."

"Oh, you're married."

"Worse than that," he said.

"What, then?"

"No time now. I can feel its approach," he said.

"What's approach?"

"The guisel," he said. "I sent one to slay another sorcerer, but he disposed of it and sent one of his own after me. Didn't know he was that good. I don't know how to dispose of the things, and it will be oozing through that mirror in a matter of minutes, to destroy us all most nastily. So, this place being Amber and all, is there some hero available who might be anxious to earn another merit badge?"

"I think not," she replied. "Sorry."

Just then the mirror began to darken.

"Oh, it's coming!" he cried.

I had felt the menace it exuded some time before. But then, that is my job.

Now I got a glimpse of the thing. It was big, and wormlike, eyeless, but possessed of a shark-like mouth, a multitude of short legs, and vestigial wings. It was twice again the length of a human, and black, having crisscrossing red

60

and yellow stripes. It slithered across our reflected room, rearing as it came on.

"You imply," Flora said, "in your quest for a hero, that it will make it through that interface and attack us?"

"In a word," said the strange little man, "yes."

When it does, I said to Flora, *throw me at it. Wherever I hit I'll stick—and I'll go for the throat.*

"All right," she said, "and there's one other thing."

What's that? I asked.

"Help! Help!" she cried.

It began crawling out through the silver, flower-bordered mirror. Flora unwound me from her ankle and threw me at the thing. It had no real neck, but I wrapped myself about its upper extremity below the mouth and began tightening immediately.

Flora continued to call out, and from somewhere up the hall I heard the sound of heavy footfalls.

I tightened my grip, but the creature's neck was like rubber.

The sorcerer was moving to exit the room when the door burst open and the tall and husky, red-haired form of Luke entered.

"Flora!" he said, and then he saw the guisel and drew his blade.

On my recent journey with Merlin in the space between shadows I had gained the ability to converse at complex levels. My perceptions—which seem quite different—also became more acute. They showed me nothing special about Luke, the sorcerer, or the guisel, but Werewindle now burned of an entirely different light. I realized then that it was not merely a blade.

As Luke moved to position himself between Flora and the guisel, I heard the sorcerer say, "What is that blade?"

"'Tis called Werewindle," Luke replied.

"And you are . . . ?"

"Rinaldo, King of Kashfa," Luke said.

"Your father—who was he?"

"Brand—Prince of Amber."

"Of course," the sorcerer said, moving again toward the door. "You can destroy that thing with it. Command it to draw energy while you're using it. It has a virtually limitless supply to draw upon."

"Why?" Luke asked.

"Because it isn't really a sword."

"What is it then?"

"Sorry," the sorcerer said, regarding the guisel, which was now moving toward us. "Out of time. Got to find another mirror."

I could tell that he was, unaware of my presence, really teasing Luke, because I had figured it out for myself and knew it would take only a moment to tell him, if one could speak.

Then I was disengaging and dropping as fast as I could, for Luke was swinging Werewindle, and I'd no desire to be severed. I really did not know what would happen if this were to occur—if both segments would wind up as wise, witty, and conscious as myself; or, perhaps, whether I would be destroyed in the process. And having no desire to learn this information firsthand, flight seemed most prudent.

I hit the floor before the blow fell. A section of the guisel's head also dropped, still writhing. I squirmed toward Luke's nearest ankle. Flora picked up a heavy chair and brought it down on the thing's back with considerable force, despite her broken fingernail. And she swung it a couple of more times, with some effect, while Luke was in the process of cutting it in half.

I found my way to where I was headed, crawled up, and caught hold.

Can you hear me, Luke? I tried then.

"Yes," he replied. "What are you?"

Merlin's strangling cord, Frakir.

Luke swung at the hind section then as it whipped toward him, tiny legs clawing. Then he whirled and halved the attacking forepart. Flora struck its rear end again with the chair.

I know what the sorcerer knew, I said.

"Oh, what's that?" he asked, slicing off another section and slipping on its gooey exudation as he retreated.

You might well be able to draw enough energy through Werewindle to destroy a world.

"Really?" he said, struggling to regain his feet as a section of the creature thrust itself upon him. "All right."

He touched it with the point of his blade and it withdrew from him as if shocked. Then he rose to his feet.

"You're right," he said. "There's something to it." He touched the attacking segment again and it vanished in a burst of blue fire. "Flora! Get back!" he cried.

She did, and he proceeded to incinerate the section that had been about to attack her. Then another that came at him.

"I'm getting the hang of it," he said, turning to get another segment. "But I'm not quite sure why it works this way."

It's not just a sword, I said.

"What is it, then?"

Long before there was Werewindle, it was the spikard Rawg.

"Spikard? Like that strange ring Merlin picked up?"

Exactly.

With rapid moves then, Luke disposed of the rest of the guisel.

"Thanks, Frakir," he said, "for telling me how the thing worked. I'd better try a quick search for that sorcerer now, though I've a hunch he disappeared into the nearest mirror."

I'd guess that, too.

"What was his name?"

He didn't say.

"It figures."

"Flora," he continued, "I'm going to look for that sorcerer. I'll be back in a bit. Good show."

She gave him a smile and he departed. Needless to say, the sorcerer did not turn up.

"Wonder where he came from, beyond the mirror," Luke asked.

I've no idea, I replied. *I think I might be more interested in the person who sent that thing after him.*

Luke nodded.

"What now?" he asked.

I guess we tell Flora that her Peeping Tom has hit the road, I said. *You're a sorcerer. Any way of fixing her mirrors so he can't pull that routine again?*

"I think so," Luke said, moving to the nearest window and looking out. "I'll fix them in just a bit. What about you?"

I'd like to get back to Merlin.

"I can't send you through by Trumps if he's in the Courts—and I suspect he is."

What about Werewindle?

"I still don't know exactly how it works. I'm going to have to practice some with it."

Uh—why are you here? I asked.

"Had to talk to Vialle about a number of things," he said, "and she told me that Corwin might be by soon—and she offered me room and board if I wanted to wait for him for a few days."

Well, if you can wear me till he gets here maybe I can persuade him to take me with him. I've a feeling he'll be seeing Merlin again soon.

"I might, too, but it's hard to say at this point."

Okay. We can work it out when the time comes.

"What do you think is going on, anyway?"

Some horrible Wagnerian thing, I told him, *full of blood, thunder, and death for us all.*

"Oh, the usual," Luke said.

Exactly, I replied.

Hall of Mirrors

Neither of us realized there had been a change until a halfdozen guys tried an ambush.

We had spent the night in the Dancing Mountains, Shask and I, where I'd witnessed a bizarre game between Dworkin and Suhuy. I'd heard strange tales about things that happened to people who spent the night there, but I hadn't had a hell of a lot of choice in the matter. It had been storming, I was tired, and my mount had become a statue. I don't know how that game turned out, though I was mentioned obliquely as a participant and I'm still wondering.

The next morning my blue horse Shask and I had crossed the Shadow Divide 'twixt Amber and Chaos. Shask was a Shadow mount my son Merlin had found for me in the royal stables of the Courts. At the moment, Shask was traveling under the guise of a giant blue lizard, and we were singing songs from various times and places.

Two men rose on either side of the trail from amid rocky cover, pointing crossbows at us. Two more stepped out before us—one with a bow, the other bearing a rather beautiful looking blade, doubtless stolen, considering the guy's obvious profession.

"Halt! and no harm'll happen," said the swordsman.

I drew rein.

"When it comes to money, I'm pretty much broke right now," I said, "and I doubt any of you could ride my mount, or would care to."

"Well now, maybe and maybe not," said the leader, "but it's a rough way to make a living, so we take whatever we can."

"It's not a good idea to leave a man with nothing," I said. "Some people hold grudges."

"Most of them can't walk out of here."

"Sounds like a death sentence to me."

He shrugged.

"That sword of yours looks pretty fancy," he said. "Let's see it."

"I don't think that's a good idea," I said.

"Why not?"

"If I draw it, I may wind up killing you," I said.

He laughed.

"We can take it off your body," he said, glancing to his right and left.

"Maybe," I said.

"Let's see it."

"If you insist."

I drew Grayswandir with a singing note. It persisted, and the eyes of the swordsman before me widened as it went on to describe an arc calculated to intersect with his neck. His own weapon came out as mine passed through his neck and continued. His cut toward Shask and passed through the animal's shoulder. Neither blow did any damage whatsoever.

"You a sorcerer?" he asked as I swung again, delivering a blow that might have removed his arm. Instead, it passed harmlessly by.

"Not the kind who does things like this. You?"

"No," he answered, striking again. "What's going on?"

I slammed Grayswandir back into the scabbard.

"Nothing," I said. "Go bother someone else."

I shook the reins, and Shask moved forward.

"Shoot him down!" the man cried.

The men on either side of the trail released their crossbow bolts, as did the other man before me. All four bolts from the sides passed through Shask, three of the men injuring or killing their opposite numbers. The one from ahead passed through me without pain or discomfort. An attempted sword blow achieved nothing for my first assailant.

"Ride on," I said.

Shask did so and we ignored their swearing as we went.

"We seem to have come into a strange situation," I observed.

The beast nodded.

"At least it kept us out of some trouble," I said.

"Funny. I'd a feeling you would have welcomed trouble," Shask said.
I chuckled.

"Perhaps, perhaps not," I replied. "I wonder how long the spell lasts?"

"Maybe it has to be lifted."

"Shit! That's always a pain."

"Beats being insubstantial."

"True."

"Surely someone back at Amber will know what to do."

"Hope so."

We rode on, and we encountered no one else that day. I felt the rocks beneath me when I wrapped myself in my cloak to sleep that night. Why did I feel them when I didn't feel a sword or a crossbow bolt? Too late to ask Shask whether he had felt anything, for he had turned to stone for the night.

I yawned and stretched. A partly unsheathed Grayswandir felt normal beneath my fingers. I pushed it back in and went to sleep.

Following my morning ablutions, we rode again. Shask was taking well to hellrides, as well as most Amber mounts did. Better, in some ways. We raced through a wildly changing landscape. I thought ahead to Amber, and I thought back to the time I'd spent imprisoned in the Courts. I had honed my sensitivity to a very high degree through meditation, and I began to wonder whether that, coupled with other strange disciplines I'd undertaken, could have led to my intangibility. I supposed it might have contributed, but I'd a feeling the Dancing Mountains were the largest donor.

"I wonder what it represents and where it came from?" I said aloud.

"Your homeland, I'd bet," Shask replied, "left especially for you."

"Why did you read it that way?"

"You've been telling me about your family as we rode along. I wouldn't trust them."

"Those days are past."

"Who knows what might have happened while you were away? Old habits return easily."

"One would need a reason for something like that."

"For all you know, one of them has a very good one."

"Possibly. But it doesn't seem likely. I've been away for some time, and few know I'm free at last."

"Then question those few."

"We'll see."

"Just trying to be helpful."

"Don't stop. Say, what do you want to do after we get to Amber?"

"Haven't made up my mind yet. I've been something of a wanderer."

I laughed.

"You're a beast after my own heart. In that your sentiments are most unbeastlike, how can I repay you for this transport?"

"Wait. I've a feeling the Fates will take care of that."

"So be it. In the meantime, though, if you happen to think of something special, let me know."

"It's a privilege to help you, Lord Corwin. Let it go at that."

"All right. Thanks."

We passed through shadow after shadow. Suns ran backward and storms assailed us out of beautiful skies. We toyed with night, which might have trapped a less adroit pair than us, found a twilight, and took our rations there. Shortly thereafter, Shask turned back to stone. Nothing attacked us that night, and my dreams were hardly worth dreaming.

Next day we were on our way early, and I used every trick I knew to shortcut us through Shadow on our way home. Home . . . It did feel good to be headed back, despite Shask's comments on my relatives. I'd no idea I would miss Amber as much as I had. I'd been away far longer on countless occasions, but usually I had at least a rough idea as to when I might be heading back. A prison in the Courts, though, was not a place from which one might make such estimates.

So we tore on, wind across a plain, fire in the mountains, water down a steep ravine. That evening I felt the resistance begin, the resistance which comes when one enters that area of Shadow near to Amber. I tried to make it all the way but failed. We spent that night at a place near to where the

Black Road used to run. There was no trace of it now.

The next day the going was slower, but, more and more, familiar shadows cropped up. That night we slept in Arden, but Julian did not find us. I either dreamed his hunting horn or heard it in the distance as I slept; and though it is often prelude to death and destruction, it merely made me feel nostalgic. I was finally near to home.

The next morning I woke before sunup. Shask, of course, was still a blue lizard curled at the base of a giant tree. So I made tea and ate an apple afterward. We were low on provisions but should soon be in the land of plenty.

Shask slowly unwound as the sun came up. I fed him the rest of the apples and gathered my possessions.

We were riding before too long, slow and easy, since there would be some hard climbing up the back route I favored. During our first break I asked him to become once more a horse, and he obliged. It didn't seem to make that much difference, and I requested he maintain it. I wanted to display his beauty in that form.

"Will you be heading right back after you've seen me here?" I asked.

"I've been meaning to talk to you about that," he responded. "Things have been slow back in the Courts, and I'm no one's assigned mount."

"Oh?"

"You're going to need a good mount, Lord Corwin."

"Yes, I'm sure."

"I'd like to apply for the job, for an indefinite period."

"I'd be honored," I said. "You're very special."

"Yes, I am."

We were atop Kolvir that afternoon and onto the grounds of Amber Palace within hours after that. I found Shask a good stall, groomed him, fed him, and left him to turn to stone at his leisure. I found a nameplate, scratched Shasko's name and my own upon it, and tacked it to his door.

"See you later," I said.

"Whatever, Lord. Whatever."

Seven Tales in Amber

I departed the stables and headed for the palace. It was a damp, cloudy day, with a chill breeze from the direction of the sea. So far, no one had spotted me.

I entered by way of the kitchen, where there was new help on duty. None of them recognized me, though they obviously realized that I belonged. At least, they returned my greeting with due respect and did not object to some fruit I pocketed. They did ask whether I cared to have something sent to one of the rooms, and I answered "yes" and told them to send a bottle of wine and a chicken along with it. The afternoon head chef—a red-haired lady named Clare—began studying me more closely, and more than once her gaze drifted toward the silver rose on my cloak. I did not want to announce my identity just then, and I thought they'd be a little afraid to guess ahead at it, at least for a few hours. I did want the time to rest a bit and just enjoy the pleasure of being back. So, "Thanks," I said, and I went on my way to my quarters.

I started up the back stairs the servants use for being unobtrusive and the rest of us for being sneaky.

Partway up, I realized that the way was blocked by sawhorses. Tools lay scattered about the stairs though there were no workmen in sight—and I couldn't tell whether a section of old stair had simply given way or whether some other force had been brought to bear upon it.

I returned, cut around to the front, and took the big stairway up. As I made my way, I saw signs of exterior repair work, including entire walls and sections of flooring. Any number of apartments were open to viewing. I hurried to make sure that mine was not among their number.

Fortunately, it was not. I was about to let myself in when a big redhaired fellow turned a corner and headed toward me. I shrugged. Some visiting dignitary, no doubt . . . .

"Corwin!" he called out. "What are you doing here?"

As he drew nearer, I saw that he was studying me most intently. I gave him the same treatment.

"I don't believe I've had the pleasure," I said.

"Aw, come on, Corwin," he said. "You surprised me. Thought you were off by your Pattern and the '57 Chevy."

I shook my head.

"Not sure what you're talking about," I said.

He narrowed his eyes.

"You're not a Pattern ghost?" he said.

"Merlin told me something about them," I said, "after he effected my release at the Courts. But I don't believe I've ever met one."

I rolled up my left sleeve.

"Cut me. I bleed," I said.

As he studied my arm, his gaze appeared more than a little serious. For a moment, I thought he'd actually take me up on it.

"All right," he said then. "Just a nick. For security purposes."

"I still don't know who I'm talking to," I said.

He bowed.

"Sorry. I am Luke of Kashfa, sometimes known as Rinaldo I, its king. If you are who you say you are, I am your nephew. My dad was your brother Brand."

Studying him, I saw the resemblance. I thrust my arm farther forward.

"Do it," I said.

"You're serious."

"Dead right."

He drew a Bowie knife from his belt then and looked into my eyes. I nodded. He moved to touch my forearm with its tip and nothing happened. That is to say, something happened, but it was neither desired nor wholly anticipated.

The point of his blade seemed to sink a half-inch or so into my arm. It kept going then, finally passing all the way through. But no blood came.

He tried again. Nothing.

"Damn," he said. "I don't understand. If you were a Pattern ghost, we'd at least get a flare. But there's not even a mark on you."

"May I borrow the blade?" I asked.

"Sure."

He passed it to me. I took it in my hand and studied it, I pushed it into my arm and drew it along for perhaps threequarters of an inch. Blood oozed.

"I'll be damned," Luke said. "What's going on?"

"I'd say it's a spell I picked up when I spent a night in the Dancing Mountains recently," I replied.

"Hm," Luke mused, "I've never had the pleasure, but I've heard stories of the place. I don't know any simple ways to break its spells. My room's off toward the front." He gestured southward. "If you'd care to stop by, I'll see what I can figure out about it. I studied Chaos magic with my dad, and with my mother, Jasra."

I shrugged.

"This is my room right here," I said, "and I've a chicken and a bottle of wine on the way up. Let's do the diagnosis in here, and I'll split the meal with you."

He smiled.

"Best offer I've had all day," he said. "But let me stop back at my room for some tools of the trade."

"All right. I'll walk you back, so I'll know the way in case I need it."

He nodded and turned. We headed up the hall.

Turning the corner, we moved from west to east, passing Flora's apartments and moving in the direction of some of the better visitors' quarters. Luke halted before one room and reached into his pocket, presumably after the key. Then he halted.

"Uh, Corwin?" he said.

"What?" I responded.

"Those two big cobrashaped candle holders," he said, gesturing up the hall. "Bronze, I believe."

"Most likely. What of them?"

"I thought they were just hall decorations."

"That's what they are."

"The last time I looked at them, they kind of bracketed a small painting or tapestry," he said.

"My recollection, too," I said.

"Well, there seems to be a corridor between them now."

"No, that can't be. There's a proper hallway just a little beyond—" I began. Then I shut up because I knew. I began walking toward it.

"What's going on?" Luke asked.

"It's calling me," I said. "I've got to go and see what it wants."

"What is it?"

"The Hall of Mirrors. It comes and goes. It brings sometimes useful, sometimes ambiguous messages to the one it calls."

"Is it calling us both, or just you?" Luke said.

"Dunno," I replied. "I feel it calling me, as it has in the past. You're welcome to come with me. Maybe it has some goodies for you, too."

"You ever hear of two people taking it at once?"

"No, but there's a first time for everything," I said.

Luke nodded slowly.

"What the hell," he said, "I'm game."

He followed me to the place of the snakes, and we peered up it. Candles flared along its walls, at either hand. And the walls glittered from the countless mirrors which hung upon them. I stepped forward. Luke followed, at my left.

The mirror frames were of every shape imaginable. I walked very slowly, observing the contents of each one. I told Luke to do the same. For several paces, the mirrors seemed simply to be giving back what was before them. Then Luke stiffened and halted, head turning to the left.

"Mom!" he said explosively.

The reflection of an attractive red-haired woman occupied a mirror framed in green-tinged copper in the shape of an Ouroboros serpent.

She smiled.

"So glad you did the right thing, taking the throne," she said.

"You really mean that?" he asked.

"Of course," she replied.

"Thought you might be mad. Thought you wanted it," he said.

"I did once, but those damned Kashfans never appreciated me. I've got the Keep now, though, and I feel like doing a few years' research here—and it's full of sentimental values as well. So as long as Kashfa stays in the family, I wanted you to know I was pleased."

"Why—uh—glad to hear that, Mom. Very glad. I'll hang onto it."

"Do," she said, and vanished.

He turned to me, a small ironic smile flickering across his lips.

"That's one of the rare times in my life when she's approved of something I've done," he said. "Doubtless for all the wrong reasons, but still . . . How real are these things? What exactly did we see? Was that a conscious communication on her part? Was—"

"They're real," I said. "I don't know how or why or what part of the other is actually present. They may be stylized, surreal, may even suck you in. But in some way they're really real. That's all I know. Holy cow!"

From the huge gold-framed mirror, ahead and to my right, the grim visage of my father Oberon peered forth. I advanced a pace.

"Corwin," he said. "You were my chosen, but you always had a way of disappointing me."

"That's the breaks," I said.

"True. And one should not speak of you as a child after all these years. You've made your choices. Of some I have been proud. You have been valiant."

"Why, thank you—sir."

"I bid you do something immediately."

"What?"

"Draw your dagger and stab Luke."

I stared.

"No," I said.

"Corwin," Luke said. "It could be something like your proving you're not a Pattern ghost."

"But I don't give a damn whether you're a Pattern ghost," I said. "It's nothing to me."

"Not that," Oberon interjected. "This is of a different order."

"What, then?" I asked.

"Easier to show than to tell," Oberon replied.

Luke shrugged.

"So nick my arm," he said. "Big deal."

"All right. Let's see how the show beats the tell."

I drew a stiletto from my boot sheath. He pulled back his sleeve and extended his arm. I stabbed lightly.

My blade passed through his arm as if the limb were made of smoke.

"Shit," Luke said. "It's contagious."

"No," Oberon responded. "It is a thing of very special scope."

"That is to say?" Luke asked.

"Would you draw your sword, please?"

Luke nodded and drew a familiar-looking golden blade. It emitted a high keening sound, causing all of the candle flames in the vicinity to flicker. Then I knew it for what it was—my brother Brand's blade, Werewindle.

"Haven't seen that in a long while," I said, as the keening continued.

"Luke, would you cut Corwin with your blade, please?"

Luke raised his eyes, met my gaze. I nodded. He moved the blade, scored my arm with its point. I bled.

"Corwin—If you would . . . ?" Oberon said.

I drew Grayswandir and it, too, ventured into fighting song—as I had only heard it do on great battlefields in the past. The two tones joined together into a devastating duet.

"Cut Luke."

Luke nodded and I sliced the back of his hand with Grayswandir. An incision line occurred, reddening immediately. The sounds from our blades rose and fell. I sheathed Grayswandir to shut her up. Luke did the same with Werewindle.

"There's a lesson there somewhere," Luke said. "Damned If I can see what it is, though."

"They're brother and sister weapons, you know, with a certain magic in common. In fact, they've a powerful secret in common," Oberon said. "Tell him, Corwin."

"It's a dangerous secret, sir."

"The time has come for it to be known. You may tell him,"

"All right," I said. "Back in the early days of creation, the gods had a series of rings their champions used in the stabilization of Shadow."

"I know of them," Luke said. "Merlin wears a spikard."

"Really," I said. "They each have the power to draw on many sources in many shadows. They're all different."

"So Merlin said."

"Ours were turned into swords, and so they remain."

"Oh?" Luke said. "What do you know?"

"What do you deduce from the fact that they can do you harm when another weapon cannot?"

"Looks as if they're somehow involved in our enchantment," I ventured.

"That's right," Oberon said. "In whatever conflict lies ahead—no matter what side you are on—you will need exotic protection against the oddball power of someone like Jurt."

"Jurt?" I said.

"Later," Luke told me. "I'll fill you in."

I nodded.

"Just how is this protection to be employed? How do we get back to full permeability?" I asked.

"I will not say," he replied, "but someone along the way here should be able to tell you. And whatever happens, my blessing—which is probably no longer worth much—lies on both of you."

We bowed and said thanks. When we looked up again, he was gone.

"Great," I said. "Back for less than an hour and involved in Amber ambiguity."

Luke nodded.

"Chaos and Kashfa seem just as bad, though," he said. "Maybe the state's highest function is to grind out insoluble problems."

I chuckled as we moved on, regarding ourselves in dozens of pools of light. For several paces nothing happened, then a familiar face appeared in a red-framed oval to my left.

"Corwin, what a pleasure," she said.

"Dara!"

"It seems that my unconscious will must be stronger than that of anyone else who wishes you ill," she said. "So I get to deliver the best piece of news of all."

"Yes?" I said.

"I see one of you lying pierced by the blade of the other. What joy!"

"I've no intention of killing this guy," I told her.

"Goes both ways," Luke said.

"Ah, but that is the deadly beauty of it," she said. "One of you must be run through by the other for the survivor to regain that element of permeability he has lost."

"Thanks, but I'll find another way," Luke said. "My mom, Jasra, is a pretty good sorceress."

Her laughter sounded like the breaking of one of the mirrors.

"Jasra! She was one of my maids," she said. "She picked up whatever she knows of the Art by eavesdropping on my work. Not without talent, but she never received full training."

"My dad completed her training," Luke said.

As she studied Luke, the merriment went out of her face.

"All right," she said. "I'll level with you, son of Brand. I can't see any way to resolve it other than the way I stated. As I have nothing against you, I hope to see you victorious."

"Thanks," he said, "but I've no intention of fighting my uncle. Someone must be able to lift this thing."

"The tools themselves have drawn you into this," she said. "They will force you to fight. They are stronger than mortal sorcery."

"Thanks for the advice," he said. "Some of it may come in handy," and he winked at her. She blushed, hardly a response I'd have anticipated, then she was gone.

"I don't like the tenor this has acquired," I said.

"Me neither. Can't we just turn around and go back?"

I shook my head.

"It sucks you in," I told him. "Just get everything you can out of it—that's the best advice I ever got on the thing."

We walked on for perhaps ten feet, past some absolutely lovely examples of mirror making as well as some battered old looking glasses.

A yellow-lacquered one on Luke's side, embossed with Chinese characters and chipped here and there, froze us in our tracks as the booming voice of my late brother Eric rang out:

"I see your fates," he said with a rumbling laugh. "And I can see the killing ground where you are destined to enact them. It will be interesting, brother. If you hear laughter as you lie dying, it will be mine."

"Oh, you always were a great kidder," I said. "By the way, rest in peace. You're a hero, you know."

He studied my face.

"Crazy brother," he said, and he turned his head away and was gone.

"That was Eric, who reigned briefly as king here?" Luke asked.

I nodded. "Crazy brother," I said.

We moved forward and a slim hand emerged from a steel-framed mirror patterned with roses of rust.

I halted, then turned quickly, somehow knowing even before I saw her who I would behold.

"Deirdre . . ." I said.

"Corwin," she replied softly.

"Do you know what's been going on as we walked along?"

She nodded.

"How much is bullshit and how much is true?" I asked.

"I don't know, but I don't think any of the others do either—not for sure."

"Thanks. I'll take all the reassurances I can get. What now?"

"If you will take hold of the other's arm, it will make the transport easier."

"What transport?"

"You may not leave this hall on your own motion. You will be taken direct to the killing ground."

"By you, love?"

"I've no choice in the matter."

I nodded. I took hold of Luke's arm.

"What do you think?" I asked him.

"I think we should go," he said, "offering no resistance—and when we find out who's behind this, we take him apart with hot irons."

"I like the way you think," I said. "Deirdre, show us the way."

"I've bad feelings about this one, Corwin."

"If, as you said, we've no choice in the matter, what difference does it make? Lead on, lady. Lead on."

She took my hand. The world began to spin around us.

Somebody owed me a chicken and a bottle of wine. I would collect.

I awoke lying in what seemed a glade under a moonlit sky. I kept my eyes half-lidded and did not move. No sense in giving away my wakefulness.

Very slowly, I moved my eyes. Deirdre was nowhere in sight. My rightside peripheral vision informed me that there might be a bonfire in that direction, with some folks seated around it.

I rolled my eyes to the left and got a glimpse of Luke. No one else seemed to be nearby.

"You awake?" I whispered.

"Yeah," he replied.

"No one near," I said, rising, "except maybe for a few around a fire off to the right. We might be able to find a way out and take it—Trumps, Shadowalk—and thus break the ritual. Or we might be trapped."

Luke put a finger into his mouth, removed it, and raised it, as if testing the wind.

"We're caught up in a sequence I think we need," he said.

"To the death?" I said.

"I don't know. But I don't really think we can escape this one," he replied. He rose to his feet.

"Ain't the fighting, it's the familiarity," I said. "I begrudge knowing you."

"Me, too. Want to flip a coin?" he asked.

"Heads, we walk away. Tails, we go over and see what the story is."

"Fine with me." He plunged his hand into a pocket, pulled out a quarter.

"Do the honors," I said.

He flipped it. We both dropped to our knees.

"Tails," he said. "Best two out of three?"

"Naw," I said. "Let's go."

Luke pocketed his quarter, and we turned and walked toward the fire.

"Only a dozen people or so. We can take them," Luke said softly.

"They don't look particularly hostile," I said.

"True."

I nodded as we approached and addressed them in Thari:

"Hello," I said. "I'm Corwin of Amber and this is Rinaldo I, King of Kashfa, also known as Luke. Are we by any chance expected here?"

An older man, who had been seated before the fire and poking at it with a stick, rose to his feet and bowed.

"My name is Reis," he said, "and we are witnesses."

"For whom?" Luke said.

"We do not know their names. There were two and they wore hoods. One, I think, was a woman. We may offer you food and drink before things begin . . . . "

"Yeah," I said, "I'm out a meal because of this. Feed me."

"Me, too," Luke added, and the man and a couple of his cohorts brought meat, apples, cheese, bread, and cups of red wine.

As we ate, I asked Reis, "Can you tell me how this thing works?"

"Of course," he said. "They told me. When you're finished eating, if you two will move to the other side of the fire, the cues will come to you."

I laughed and then I shrugged.

"All right," I said.

Finished dining, I looked at Luke. He smiled.

"If we've got to sing for our supper," Luke said, "let's give them a ten-minute demonstration and call it a draw."

I nodded.

"Sounds good to me."

We put aside our plates, rose, moved to the fire, and passed behind it.

"Ready?" I said.

"Sure. Why not?"

We drew our weapons, stepped back, and saluted. We both laughed when the music began. Suddenly, I found myself attacking, though I had decided to await the attack and put my first energies into its counter. The movement had been thoughtless, though quite deft and speedy.

"Luke," I said as he parried, "it got away from me. Be careful. There's something odd going on."

"I know," he said as he delivered a formidable attack. "I wasn't planning that."

I parried it and came back even faster. He retreated.

"Not bad," he said, as I felt something loosened in my arm. Suddenly I was fencing on my own again, voluntarily, with no apparent control but with fear that it might be reasserted at any moment.

Suddenly, I knew that we were fairly free and it scared me. If I weren't sufficiently vicious, I might be taken over again. If I were, someone might slip in an unsolicited move at the wrong moment. I grew somewhat afraid.

"Luke, if what's happening to you is similar to what's been happening to me, I don't like this show a bit," I told him.

"Me neither," he said.

I glanced back across the fire. A pair of hooded individuals stood among the others. They were not overlarge and there was a certain whiteness within the cowl of the nearer.

"We've more audience," I said.

Luke glanced back; it was only with great difficulty that I halted a cowardly attack as he turned away. When we returned to hard combat, he shook his head.

"Couldn't recognize either of them," he said. "This seems a little more serious than I thought."

"Yeah."

"We can both take quite a beating and recover."

"True."

Our blades rattled on. Occasionally, one or the other of us received a cheer.

"What say we injure each other," Luke said, "then throw ourselves down and wait for their judgment on whatever's been accomplished. If either of them come near enough, we take them out just for laughs."

"Okay," I said. "If you can expose your left shoulder a bit, I'm willing to take a midline cut. Let's give them lots of gore before we flop, though. Head and forearm cuts. Anything easy."

"Okay. And 'simultaneity' is the word."

So we fought. I stood off a bit, going faster and faster. Why not? It was kind of a game.

Suddenly, my body executed a move I had not ordered it to. Luke's eyes widened as the blood spurted and Grayswandir passed entirely through his shoulder. Moments later, Werewindle pierced my vitals.

"Sorry," Luke said. "Listen, Corwin. If you live and I don't, you'd better know that there's too much crazy stuff involving mirrors going on around the castle. The night before you came back, Flora and I fought a creature that came out of a mirror. And there's an odd sorcerer involved—has a crush on Flora. Nobody knows his name. Has something to do with Chaos, though, I'd judge. Could it be that for the first time Amber is starting to reflect Shadow, rather than the other way around?"

"Hello," said a familiar voice. "The deed is done."

"Indeed," said another.

It was the two cowled figures who had spoken. One was Fiona, the other Mandor.

"However it be resolved, good night, sweet prince," said Fiona.

I tried to rise. So did Luke. Tried also to raise my blade. Could not. Again, the world grew dim, and this time I was leaking precious bodily fluids.

"I'm going to live—and come after you," I said.

"Corwin," I heard her say faintly. "We are not as culpable as you may think. This was—"

"—all for my own good, I'll bet," I muttered before the world went dark, growling with the realization that I hadn't gotten to use my death curse. One of these days . . . .

I woke up in the dispensary in Amber, Luke in the next bed. We both had IVs dripping into us.

"You're going to live," Flora said, lowering my wrist from taking my pulse. "Care to tell me your story now?"

"They just found us in the hall?" Luke asked. "The Hall of Mirrors was nowhere in sight?"

"That's right."

"I don't want to mention any names yet," I said.

"Corwin," Luke said, "Did the Hall of Mirrors show up a lot when you were a kid?"

"No," I said.

"Hardly ever, when I was growing up either," Flora said. "It's only in recent years that it's become this active. Almost as if the place were waking up."

"The place?" Luke said.

"Almost as if there's another player in the game," she responded.

"Who?" I demanded, causing a pain in my gut.

"Why, the castle itself, of course," she said.

Made in the USA
Coppell, TX
13 March 2021

51706250R00052